A SUMMER OF DISCOVERY

AMISH BONNET SISTERS: LEGACY OF FAITH
BOOK ONE

SAMANTHA PRICE

Copyright © 2025 by Samantha Price

All rights reserved.

No part of this book may be reproduced in any form or by any electronic or mechanical means, including information storage and retrieval systems, without written permission from the author, except for the use of brief quotations in a book review.

CHAPTER 1

IRIS SLIPPED QUIETLY onto the porch, tiptoeing to the kitchen window. Pressing her ear to the cool glass, she strained to catch her parents' conversation.

Their voices floated through a small crack in the window, just enough for her to piece together what they were saying. She held her breath, willing them to agree to her plan. They had to understand. They just had to.

The first voice she heard was her mothers. "Carter, she's been talking about this since she was a little girl. It's not some whim. Iris feels a strong pull toward the community, and you know that."

Her father's sigh was audible, followed by the sound of his chair scraping as he shifted. "I'm not saying it's a whim. But staying with your mother all summer? That's a big step for someone who's only eighteen. And isn't Ada's nephew still staying with Wilma?"

"Mathew's there, but he'll be gone soon."

Her father hesitated. "But what if she decides not to come back? Have you thought about that? She's eighteen and that's old enough to do what she wants."

"I know."

"Well, prepare yourself."

There was a brief silence before her mother replied. "If we don't let her go now, she might make a rash decision later. You know how she is when she feels stifled."

Iris's jaw dropped. Stifled? When had she ever acted rashly?

"I just think it's too soon," her father continued. "She needs to think about her future, about what she's really giving up if she chooses to join the Amish community. She hasn't experienced enough of life to know. Perhaps if we hadn't home schooled her she would've experienced more…"

"More of what?" Florence asked.

"More of what life could offer her."

Iris knew exactly what she wanted. The Amish way of life had fascinated her since childhood, ever since those long summer days spent with her grandmother, watching her work in the garden, bake bread, and quilt by lamplight.

The simplicity, the quiet faith, the closeness of the community—it had all called to her in a way she couldn't explain. And now that she was old enough to make choices about her life, she wanted the chance to explore that pull.

Her mother's voice softened, but it was clear she was holding back emotion. "I left the community for you. I left everything I knew to be with you because I loved you, and I don't regret it. But this is different. Iris isn't talking about leaving us. She's not running away, she's searching for something. She's always been different from Chess, more serious, more thoughtful."

Iris bit her lip at the mention of her annoying younger brother. Chess never missed an opportunity to tease her about her interest in the Amish way of life. For him, the idea of living without technology, without freedom to do as he pleased, was a joke. He made fun of her for wanting something so 'old-fashioned,' but Iris didn't care. Chess didn't understand what it felt like to be torn between two worlds.

Her father's voice broke through her thoughts. "I get it, Florence. I really do. But she's eighteen. That's too young to be thinking about commitment to anything, let alone a life like that. And if she stays... well, what then? She could marry young, start a family. Is that what we want for her? For her to lose out on the things she could experience, the things she could become?"

Florence's voice was quieter. "What if that *is* what she wants? We can't push her into a life that's not hers, just because it's what we chose for ourselves. Iris is her own person."

There was a silence that stretched too long, and Iris could imagine her father rubbing the back of his neck, staring at the kitchen table like it held all the answers. She'd seen that look before when he had been deep in thought.

"I just want her to be sure," Carter finally said. "If she goes to live with your mother this summer, I want to know she's making this decision with her eyes open."

"She's had her eyes open for years," Florence said gently. "She thinks she knows what it means to be Amish, but maybe when she stays with Wilma she'll see it's not what she thought.."

"I see what you mean. At the moment she's looking through rose-colored glasses"

"And It's just for the summer unless she wants to come home sooner."

Iris's heart pounded. Just a summer. That's all she was asking for—a chance to live with her grandmother, to see if the life she'd dreamed of was truly the life she wanted. She didn't know what the future held, but she knew she needed to explore this part of herself before it slipped away forever.

The door behind her creaked open, and Iris jumped, spinning around to see Chess grinning at her from the doorway.

"Eavesdropping again, Iris? Geez, you're worse than a nosy old lady," he teased, his voice dripping with mockery. "What are they saying? Gonna send you off to live in some dusty old house with no Wi-Fi?"

Iris glared at him, her heart still racing from being caught. "Mind your business, Chess. You wouldn't understand, and Grandma's house is clean, not dusty. I might tell her you said that."

He stepped closer, his smirk widening. "Oh, I understand. You want to go churn butter and wear those weird dresses all summer. What a blast."

She pushed past him into the house, her temper flaring. "You don't get it because you don't care about anything but your stupid video games and your dumb friends."

Chess snorted, following her down the hallway. "Yeah, because living without electricity sounds like so much fun. You're gonna hate it. You'll be back in a week. No, in a day."

Iris spun around to face him. "I won't, Chess. I'm not like you. I don't need all this noise and distraction. I need to figure out who I am, and if that means spending the summer with Grandma, then that's exactly what I'm going to do."

Her brother blinked, taken aback by her determination, but quickly recovered with a teasing grin. "Okay, fine. But when you come back bored out of your mind, don't say I didn't warn you."

Ignoring him, Iris made her way to her room, where the quiet could finally wrap around her. She leaned against the door, closing her eyes. Her parents were still debating her future in the kitchen, but Iris knew her choice was made. This summer with Grandma could be the key to finding the path her heart had always been drawn to.

CHAPTER 2

WITH A BASKET LOOPED over her arm Wilma pushed open the wooden door of Ada's small cottage, the familiar scent of lavender greeting her as she stepped inside. Ada had moved to a small house after Samuel, her husband, died the year before. Obadiah, Wilma's third husband had died a month later. From outside, Wilma heard Ada softly humming. Wilma smiled to herself. Ada always managed to keep a sense of calm, no matter what life threw her way.

"Knock, knock," Wilma said as she entered the house.

Ada looked up from her rocking chair, her arm cradled in a sling, a half-knitted blanket draped over her lap. "Wilma! It's about time you got here. Come sit by me."

"You shouldn't be knitting with that broken arm, Ada. You'll hurt yourself more."

Ada shrugged a shoulder, dropping the needles. "I'm only balancing it with my bad arm. Besides, I've got to do something to keep busy. Sitting around doing nothing never helped anyone."

Wilma settled into the chair across from her, setting the basket of baked goods she'd brought on the table.

"Has Florence made up her mind yet?" Ada asked.

Wilma sighed, resting her hands in her lap. "Not yet. Iris has been trying to convince her, but I think Carter is the one holding back. He'd think she's too young to know what she really wants."

Ada nodded thoughtfully. "You could use the help with the house."

"I could, but now that Obadiah is gone I'm doing a whole lot less cooking. Now if you'd moved in with me like we were considering, it might be a different story."

Ada smiled. "We'll do that in our old age, Wilma. I'm not there yet. I just want to imagine that Samuel is still around and it won't be easy to do that if I'm living with you."

Wilma smiled at the mention of Ada's late husband. Samuel had been a good man, and Ada's world had been noticeably dimmer since his passing.

"I'm not a crazy person, that's just the way I feel," Ada said.

"I completely understand. I miss Obadiah as well."

Ada looked up at the ceiling as though deep in thought. "Are you ready to have Iris living with you, and is it right to have her staying there when Matthew is living with you?"

Wilma paused, thinking of her quiet home. "Of course it's appropriate. They are too far apart in age for anyone to consider they'd be interested in each other."

Ada nodded. "I guess so and they're also related with Mercy

and Honor married to his brothers. It's called being related by marriage."

Wilma laughed a little. "Let's just wait and see if Iris comes to stay with me first. I want to spend all my time with her."

"She's eighteen, Wilma. She's a young woman. I don't think she'll want to spend all her time with her grandmother."

Wilma smiled at Ada's exaggeration. "Well, she might for the first couple of weeks. She is a little shy at times. I think it'll be good for her to be with me. And it might be good for me, too. Matthew helps around the house, but I have to ask him three times before he does anything. I don't know if he's just lazy or if something's wrong with him."

Ada frowned. "What do you mean?"

"When I ask him to do something, he always says next week, or next weekend. Sometimes he says tomorrow, but you know what they say about tomorrow?"

Ada nodded. "Jah. Tomorrow never comes."

"It's never anything big, just little repairs here and there. I'm sorry, Ada. I know he's your nephew, but…"

Ada chuckled, waving her free hand. "Don't be sorry. I have to agree with you. Matthew's always been a little slow to act. I mean, look how he's treated poor Grace over the years. I don't know why he just doesn't marry her and be done with it."

"It's probably time for her to forget about him," Wilma said.

"But love's not so easy to forget, Wilma." Ada's voice was soft which was so unlike her.

Wilma's heart tightened at her words, and the sting of unshed tears burned the back of her eyes. She turned her face away from Ada, her vision blurring slightly as she blinked hard against the rising emotions. She was no stranger to love, or to loss. She'd buried three husbands, each one leaving a different scar on her heart.

The community had whispered behind her back after the second, and when the third had passed, some had dared to call her cursed. But Wilma knew the truth. God gave and took away, and love—well, love left behind memories too deep to fully forget.

Ada reached out with her left hand and clasped Wilma's fingers tightly. "Now don't start crying, Wilma. Or I'll start and I won't be able to stop."

Wilma managed a smile. "I've found it easier not to think about him at all."

"You're right about love. It stays with you, whether you want it to or not." Ada held her hand a moment longer, her eyes full of quiet understanding. "I guess we both know that better than most."

Wilma nodded, blinking rapidly to dispel the tears that still threatened to fall. "That we do."

The room was silent for a moment. Wilma let herself breathe in the calm, feeling the steadying presence of her old friend.

Ada changed the subject. "If they let Iris come, I think she will do well with you. She's got a good head on her shoulders, just like her grandmother. And who knows, maybe she'll be a good influence on Matthew in some way. It might force him to face what his life has become. No permanent place to live, no wife—"

"At least he has a job." Wilma chuckled, the heaviness in her heart easing just a little. "I don't know if anyone can help that young man. But I suppose… we'll see."

Ada grinned. "If anyone can, it'll be Iris. She's determined and she seems to have her mother's skills of organization. Remember how Florence had her younger sisters in line when they were all younger?"

Wilma smiled, thinking of the old days. "I just hope Iris finds what she's looking for, whatever that is."

Ada nodded in agreement. "Can you make us some tea?"

"Of course." As Wilma rose and moved to the kitchen, a light knock sounded at the door. She glanced toward the window where a familiar figure stood.

"That must be Malachi," Ada called.

"I'll get it," Wilma said, opening the door to find Malachi with his oldest son beside him, hat in hand and dark hair slightly tousled by the evening breeze.

"Hi Wilma. This is for Ada from Cherish," he said, offering a casserole dish.

Wilma took it from him. "Oh, that's very kind."

He offered a small nod. "Hi Mammi," Josiah said, smiling up at her.

"Hi there. Come in. I was just about to make tea, and I can get milk for you, Josiah."

Malachi shook his head. "Not today, thanks. We've got to go back and help with the milking, don't we?" he said, looking down at his son.

"Yep," Josiah said, a man of few words.

Ada called out, "Hello, you two."

"Hello, Ada," Malachi said, peering further into the house. "What would you like done today?"

"Actually, I could use some help with the chicken coop door. It's been sticking again," Ada said. "I think the hinges need oiling or something. I can't get chickens till it's all secure."

"I'll take care of it," Malachi said with a nod. "Anything else?"

Ada chuckled softly. "No, no. That's enough to keep you busy for now, but no need to do that today if you're in a hurry."

"I'll take a look at it and if it's a big job we'll do it tomorrow."

"Denke," Ada said as she waved to young Josiah.

Wilma watched the exchange with fondness, noting how Malachi, despite his quiet demeanor, always seemed to make sure Ada was comfortable. As he walked toward the barn, she prepared the tea and some of Cherish's casserole, bringing both on a tray to Ada.

"Tea makes everything better," Ada said, carefully taking her cup. As she looked at the heated meal, her face lit up. "That smells so good. And the bread and butter, mmm."

Wilma moved to leave. "I'll let you enjoy that in peace."

"Not before I tell you my news," Ada said, eyes twinkling. "Today I got a letter from Adaline. She's coming for a few months to look after me. We might both have our granddaughters staying with us."

Wilma swallowed hard. "Adaline? When is she coming?"

"She said this week, didn't name a day." Ada must have noticed Wilma's expression because she added, "Relax, Wilma. She's only twenty-two now, and she and Iris are just four years apart. They can spend time together when we visit - it'll be perfect."

"That is, if Carter and Florence allow Iris to come," Wilma pointed out.

"There's no question about it. I don't think Iris will accept 'no' for an answer."

Wilma picked up her basket, mind already planning tomorrow's visit. "I'll come by with more bread and tidy up a bit before she arrives."

Ada smiled warmly. "Really, there's no need. Adaline will be perfectly happy to make up her own bed. She's a very easy going person, just like me."

Wilma chuckled and turned to leave. Walking out into the fading light of the evening, she worried about Adaline's visit. She wasn't an easy person to get along with, but maybe she had changed in the two years since she'd visited. At least, Wilma hoped so.

CHAPTER 3

IRIS LEFT her bedroom and made her way to the living room. She sat on the edge of the couch, her leg bouncing restlessly as she tried to keep herself from storming into the kitchen. Her parents had been in there for what felt like hours, their voices too low for her to make out the details of the conversation.

She glanced over at Chess, who was sprawled out on the floor, flicking a piece of string back and forth, annoying her big, fat tabby cat, Romeo. The cat had been stretched out asleep, but every few minutes, his tail would twitch in irritation as Chess dangled the string near his nose.

"Leave him alone. He's trying to sleep," Iris snapped.

Chess didn't even look up. "He's fat. He could use the exercise. Anyway, I'm hungry. I hope they're cooking in there and not just talking."

Iris huffed in frustration. "All you do is eat, Chess. You eat enough for three people."

Chess smirked, flicking the string again. Romeo swiped

lazily at it, his eyes half-open, clearly annoyed. "That's 'cause I'm gonna grow up big and tall—taller than anyone in the family. Maybe even taller than Dad."

Iris couldn't take it anymore. The anxiety bubbling up inside her had reached its peak. She stood up abruptly, startling both Chess and Romeo. "I can't do this," she muttered, marching toward the kitchen. Her heart pounded in her chest, but she didn't care. She needed to know if her parents had made a decision.

Without thinking, she burst through the kitchen door, interrupting her parents mid-conversation. Her mother looked up in surprise, her eyes wide. Her father was equally shocked, the spoon in his hand hovering over a steaming pot on the stove.

"Iris!" Florence gasped. "What in the world—"

"I can't wait any longer!" Iris blurted out, her face flushed from the sudden burst of courage. "Have you made a decision?"

There was a moment of silence as her parents exchanged a glance. Iris held her breath, feeling the weight of their gaze.

Finally, her father sighed, setting down the spoon. "We've talked it over, and we've decided… we'll allow you to go. But only for the summer and then if you want to stay longer, we'll talk about it then."

A jolt of excitement shot through Iris. Her heart leaped, and before she could stop herself, she let out a squeal of joy. "Thank you! Thank you, thank you!" She was practically jumping up and down, her hands clapping together in relief.

Just then, Chess wandered into the kitchen, Romeo trailing behind him, his tail flicking in annoyance from being disturbed. Chess raised an eyebrow at the sight of Iris bouncing around like a little kid. "Calm down. It's just the summer. And anyway, now that you're eighteen, you can do anything you want. You don't need their permission."

His words hit the air like a pin in a balloon, and the room fell silent. Iris stopped her excited bouncing, her joy dampened slightly by his bluntness. She looked at her parents, hoping they'd put him in his place.

Florence was quick to respond. "Your sister respects us, Chess. That's why she's asked for our advice. Just because she's legally an adult doesn't mean she's going to stop caring about what we think."

Iris felt a surge of warmth at her mother's words. It was true. She could have pushed ahead without asking, but that wasn't how their family worked. She valued their opinions, even if she was eager to find her own way.

"Your mother is right, as usual," Carter said smiling at Florence. "While you're both under our roof, you have to follow our rules."

Chess shrugged, clearly unconcerned by what anyone said. "Yeah, well, I'm gonna do whatever I want when I'm eighteen."

Florence glared at him. "That's a long way off, young man. And right now, you can start by respecting the decisions we make for you."

Chess rolled his eyes, clearly uninterested in the lecture. "Whatever. So, what's for dinner?"

Carter chuckled, shaking his head as he lifted the pot lid. "I'm making stew. If you're that hungry, you can help me set the table."

Chess groaned, clearly not pleased with the idea of having to do any actual work. "Ugh, fine."

Iris watched the exchange as her mind buzzed with plans for

the summer. But a new thought suddenly popped into her head. "Can I take Romeo with me?"

Chess's head whipped around, and Romeo, who had been circling around Iris's legs, paused to look up at her with sleepy eyes. "You can't take *my* cat!" Chess exclaimed.

Iris scoffed, crossing her arms. "*Your* cat? Romeo's mine, and you know it."

Chess's face scrunched in disbelief. "Since when? I'm the one who feeds him. He's practically my shadow."

Iris rolled her eyes. "Yeah, because you're always dropping food everywhere. He only follows you around because you're a walking buffet."

"That's not true! Romeo likes me because I don't annoy him like you do. You're always trying to cuddle him, and he hates that."

"He does not, and what's more he sleeps on my bed every night."

"Only because I keep my door locked," Chess grumbled.

"Yeah, because you watch too many horror movies and you think someone's coming to get you."

Florence held up her hands, stepping between the two of them before the argument could escalate any further. "All right, that's enough. Romeo belongs to both of you. And Iris, you'll have to leave Romeo here. He'll be fine."

"But, Mom—" Iris began, but her mother cut her off with a gentle but firm look.

Then Carter said, "Iris, he's happy here. Chess is right, he's used to this place. It wouldn't be fair to take him away, even if it's just for the summer."

Iris frowned, glancing down at Romeo, who had now curled

up on the kitchen floor, completely uninterested in the drama swirling around him.

Chess smirked in triumph and said under his breath, "I won that one."

Iris glared at him but chose to let it go, too relieved about her summer plans to let Chess get under her skin.

For now, she had something far more exciting to look forward to.

CHAPTER 4

Wilma stood on the porch, watching the long, dusty road that stretched out from the home of the Baker Apple Orchard. She expected to see Carter's shiny black car bringing Iris.

The house had been tidied, and one of the upstairs rooms had been prepared for her granddaughter.

The distant sound of an engine broke the silence. Wilma squinted, and to her surprise, a white rental truck came into view, rumbling up the road. Then it turned into her driveway.

"What's this?" she murmured to herself, stepping down from the porch to get a closer look.

The truck pulled to a stop in front of the house, and before Wilma could fully process what she was seeing, Iris burst from the back door and ran toward her with open arms.

"Grandma!" Iris squealed as she flung her arms around her.

Wilma hugged her tightly, still eyeing the truck with confusion. "Welcome, Iris."

"Thank you. I'm so happy to be here finally."

"Why did you come in a truck?" Wilma asked.

Iris pulled back, brushing a strand of hair from her face. "Oh, I just brought some things to keep me occupied," she said with a grin. Before Wilma could ask for details, Carter jumped out of the driver's seat, and Florence climbed out from the other side, both of them already heading toward the back of the truck.

Wilma's eyes widened as she watched them unload a large, familiar object. "Is that…?"

Florence smiled apologetically as she and Carter maneuvered the old fashioned treadle sewing machine toward the house. "I hope this is all right, Wilma. Iris loves to sew, and I thought it might be a nice way for her to spend some time here. You know how much she enjoys it."

"I can sew clothes for everyone!" Iris chimed in excitedly. "I can make dresses for all my aunts and all my cousins too."

Wilma blinked, still processing the sight of it. "Well, yes, it's fine," she finally said, her voice trailing off. "But it'll need to go upstairs in one of the spare rooms. There's no space for it down here."

As they carried the sewing machine into the house, Wilma stood back.

"Grandma," Iris said, grabbing Wilma's arm gently, "we're going to have so much fun! I've brought books, fabric, my sketchpad—everything! I'll sew for you, and we can bake together, and…"

Suddenly, Matthew appeared from around the side of the house. "Need some help with that?" he asked, quickly taking over from Florence.

Florence stepped back. "Thanks, Matthew. It is rather heavy."

Wilma was amazed at how Matthew was so helpful for other people while totally avoiding anything she'd asked him to do.

With a nod from Wilma, he and Carter disappeared inside, leaving Florence and Iris outside.

"I didn't expect you to bring so much," Wilma said, shaking her head with a soft chuckle. "I thought you'd just be bringing your clothes and maybe a book or two."

"I wanted to be prepared. Besides, if I'm staying the whole summer, I'll need things to keep me busy, and sewing's my favorite. I can make you new curtains, or even a dress if you'd like. I can make clothes for the whole family."

Wilma's heart softened at Iris's enthusiasm. "Well, I suppose I can't argue with that. I always love a new dress. I hope you didn't plan on sewing every day, Iris. There's plenty to do around here that doesn't involve sitting at a machine."

"I know, I know," Iris replied, rolling her eyes playfully. "I'll help with the garden, too. I know how much you love it out there."

Wilma smiled at that. It was true—her garden was one of her greatest joys, and she often spent hours tending to it. The idea of sharing that time with Iris brought a quiet excitement to her heart. "Well, if you're serious about that, I'll hold you to it."

"Of course I'm serious. I'm looking forward to everything, and being with you." Iris slipped her hand into her grandmother's.

Wilma studied her granddaughter for a moment, feeling a surge of affection. Iris had always been independent, with a mind of her own, but there was something more mature about her now. She was no longer a little girl tagging along dressed in Amish clothes for something different; she was a young woman, ready to take on new responsibilities and explore the life she felt so drawn to.

As they stood together on the porch, Carter and Matthew came back outside. "Everything's in. I think that sewing machine will get a lot of use this summer," Carter said.

"I hope so. It'll keep her busy in the evenings."

Matthew gave Iris a small nod. "You've got a lot for just a summer, Iris."

Iris shrugged. "I like to be prepared."

"Well, you'll fit right in," Matthew said, glancing at Wilma. "Your grandma here always says there's no such thing as being too prepared."

Wilma chuckled. "He's not wrong. All right, Iris. Let's get settled and figure out where all your things will go. I'll help you unpack."

Iris took a deep breath, realizing the moment had come. Even though her parents would be right next door, she'd never had more than two nights away from them at a time. She ran up to her father, wrapping him in a tight hug. "Thanks, Dad. For everything."

Carter smiled at her. "Take care of your grandma, all right? And take care of yourself."

"I will," Iris promised before turning to her mother, who already had her arms outstretched.

Florence pulled Iris in close. "You'll be fine. Just don't forget to come visit, okay? I want to hear about everything."

"I won't forget." Saying goodbye felt harder than she'd anticipated, but the excitement for the summer ahead still pulsed through her. She stepped back and smiled, waving as her parents made their way back to the truck.

Matthew, yelled out goodbye to Florence and Carter before turning to Iris. "I'll be out with the horses if you want your sewing machine moved to the window or something."

Iris nodded. "Thanks, Matthew. I'll take a look later, it might be nice near the window."

Carter gave Iris one last wave before climbing into the truck. "Good luck, sweetheart."

Iris waved some more and then the truck pulled away.

"Come on now. Let's get you unpacked before the sun sets."

Iris nodded, following her grandmother inside and up the stairs to the spare bedroom where most of her things had been piled. The room was cozy, with a quilt-covered bed in the corner and an old-fashioned wardrobe standing against the wall.

"Let's start with the clothes," Wilma said, opening one of Iris's suitcases. "We'll get those hung up, and then we can figure out where everything else will go."

As they unpacked in silence, Iris glanced over at her grandmother. "So what's going on with Matthew? I heard he was getting married and then it never happened."

Wilma sighed deeply, setting down the hanger. She straightened up, looking out the window for a moment before turning back to Iris. "He was supposed to, a few times now. But Matthew... well, he needs help."

Iris frowned, her curiosity piqued. "Help with what? I thought everything was going fine with him and Grace."

Wilma shook her head slowly. "It's been ten years of this back-and-forth with those two. One day they're planning a future together, and the next, they're hardly speaking. I think

Grace's more tired of it than anyone, but she's too patient for her own good. Every time things fall apart, she waits around for Matthew to come to his senses."

"Ten years?" Iris said, her eyes widening. "I didn't realize it had been going on that long."

Wilma nodded, sitting down on the edge of the bed, relieved to be able to share what had been weighing on her mind. "Matthew's always been a bit slow to figure things out, even when it comes to his own feelings. I don't know if he's just scared of change or if there's something else holding him back."

Iris sat down beside her grandmother, processing the complexity of the situation. "Why doesn't Grace just realize it's not meant to be and move on? If it's been this long…"

Wilma gave her a sad smile. "Love's not always that simple, Iris. Sometimes, when your heart's set on someone, it's hard to let go, even if it's the best thing for you. Grace has had offers from other men, but she's always come back to Matthew. And every time it looks like they might finally settle down, something happens. He pulls away, or they argue, and it's back to the beginning for them."

Iris frowned. "Do you think he'll ever make up his mind?"

Wilma sighed again, her shoulders sagging a little. "I don't know which one of them is holding back. I do think it's Matthew. I've tried talking to him, tried helping him see that he should date other women, but it's like talking to a brick wall. I don't know what's going to push him out of this cycle."

Iris bit her lip. "Maybe I can help. I mean, if I'm going to be around for the summer, maybe I can talk with him and find out why they broke up. It could be something fixable."

Wilma chuckled. "Which break up are we talking about? There have been about five of them."

"Oh."

Wilma looked at her granddaughter with gratitude. "You've always had a way of getting through to people. Maybe having you around will shake things up a bit."

Iris smiled. "We'll figure it out, Grandma. I'm sure we will."

"You came here for yourself, so don't be concerned about Matthew." Wilma stood up and picked up the hanger. "We're going to have a good summer."

With that, the two of them continued unpacking, their conversation lightening as they talked about plans for the coming days. But Iris continued thinking about Matthew and Grace.

CHAPTER 5

THE NEXT MORNING, Iris was in the kitchen early. The sweet scent of maple syrup wafted through the air as she stood at the stove, humming to herself while she flipped pancakes. From her spot at the table, Wilma wrapped her hands around her coffee mug and watched her granddaughter.

"I had the best sleep. That bed is amazing. I wanted to bring my own bed and my cat too, but I didn't need to bring my bed. This bed is even better. Mom said no about the cat."

Wilma chuckled. "There was no need to bring so much. I'm glad you didn't bring the bed, but you could've brought Romeo."

"Really?" Iris turned away from the pancakes to stare at her grandmother.

"Yes, but since your mother said no we can't go against that."

"She only said that because Chess said he wanted Romeo.

He was just saying that so I wouldn't be happy. What annoys me is how he always gets his way. He's spoilt."

Wilma chuckled. "I'm sure that's not so."

"I'm sure it is so."

"I could get used to getting meals cooked for me." Wilma took a sip of coffee.

"I want to know how to cook everything you eat. I expect you to teach me all those recipes while I'm here."

Wilma chuckled. "Oh, don't worry. I've got plenty to teach. But I won't say no to having breakfast cooked for me. I take a while to get started in the mornings these days. Especially the cold mornings."

Iris turned back to the stove, and turned the pancakes. "Matthew must leave early."

"He does. He gets up at sunrise."

Suddenly, a faint tapping sound broke the calm. Iris froze, her brow furrowing as she glanced up at the window in front of her. Outside, the garden was still and quiet so she couldn't see where the noise came from.

Tap-tap-tap.

The noise came again, sharper this time. Iris leaned forward, squinting further out the window, but there was nothing there. "Grandma, do you hear that?" she asked, turning to Wilma.

"Hear what? I haven't heard anything." Wilma raised an eyebrow, setting her coffee down.

Iris frowned, turning back to the window. "There's this tapping noise. It's weird." She shook her head and went back to cooking, trying to brush off the unsettling sound. But then the tapping came again, louder and more deliberate.

"I hear it now," Wilma said.

Iris put down the spatula and stepped closer to the window, peering out to see what could be causing it.

Finally, deciding she needed to know what was going on, she unlocked the window and pushed it open. "What in the world is—"

Before she could finish, a face shot up from below the window, and Chess jumped up, shouting. "Boo!"

Iris screamed, stumbling back as she tried to catch her breath.

Chess, meanwhile, burst into laughter, practically collapsing against the windowsill. "I got you. You should've seen your face."

Her hands clenched into fists as she glared at him, her entire body trembling with frustration. "Chess! What are you doing here? You scared me half to death!"

Still chuckling, Chess clambered through the open window, landing on the kitchen floor with a thud. "I was bored. Thought I'd come over and see what you guys were up to." He smirked, clearly pleased with himself. "Didn't expect to get such a good scare in before breakfast. Ah, it's gonna be a good day."

Iris's jaw tightened as she turned her back on him, trying to suppress the urge to yell. This wasn't how she'd imagined her peaceful morning would unfold. All she wanted was a few weeks without Chess's antics.

Wilma, still sitting at the table, chuckled softly. "Oh, Chess, you certainly know how to make an entrance." She stood up and walked over to her grandson, giving him a warm smile. "Why don't you stay for breakfast? We've got plenty of food."

Iris whipped around, her eyes wide. "Grandma, no! He wasn't invited. He's not even supposed to be here."

Chess grinned, clearly enjoying her reaction as he plopped into a chair at the table. "What's the fuss? It's just breakfast."

Iris glared at Chess. "I *made* this breakfast, and you don't even live here," Iris snapped, her voice rising. "You ruin everything, Chess. You always do this—showing up when no one wants you, making everything into a joke."

Wilma looked between them, her smile fading. "Iris, that's enough. He's young and he's just being playful."

Iris shook her head, her frustration boiling over. "No, Grandma. He's always like this. Every time I try to do something, Chess shows up and ruins it."

Chess's eyes flitted from side to side as he smirked. "That's not right."

"It is. When I got on the basketball team you tried to join."

Chess chuckled. "What's wrong with that?"

"It was an all girls' team."

"Well, they should've been more inclusive." He threw his head back and laughed.

Iris looked over at Wilma for help. "I came here to spend time with you, not to deal with *him* every single day. I need a break."

His usual smug grin faltered as he glanced at Wilma looking for support.

Wilma's expression softened, and she stepped forward, placing a hand on Iris's arm. "I didn't realize you felt that way, Iris. But this is his home, too, in a way. He's family just like you are. My door is always open to both of you."

"I rest my case," Chess said.

Iris could feel her chest tightening. "He's always making it about him. I just wanted my first morning here with you, Grandma." A tear trickled down her cheek.

Seeing his sister so upset, Chess shifted uncomfortably. "I didn't mean to make you upset, Iris... I was just messing around."

Iris clenched her fists. "You *never* mean to make me upset, but you always do. It's exhausting. I came here mostly to get away from *you*."

Wilma let out a long sigh, clearly torn. "I understand you're upset, but we're all family. We'll figure this out."

Iris wiped away her tear. She couldn't deal with Chess today. Not now. She served the pancakes and then turned away from them. "I'm eating breakfast. You two can talk."

The peaceful morning she had wanted was gone, and all she could think about was how he'd ruined things for her—again.

CHAPTER 6

After Chess had gone home, it was time for chores. Iris stood in front of the large, old-fashioned wringer washer, her hands on her hips, studying it like a puzzle she wasn't entirely sure she wanted to solve. The machine whirred softly, the smell of soap and damp clothes hanging in the air.

"I don't think I've seen one of these outside of a museum," Iris said, raising an eyebrow as she looked over at Wilma, who was busy sorting the next load of laundry.

Wilma chuckled. "It might seem ancient to you, but this washing machine still gets the job done just fine. You'll get used to it."

"Used to it? I didn't even know there was a time when washing machines looked like this. I feel like I should be turning butter with it or something."

"You don't have to turn butter—yet. But let's start with the washing. Here, help me with Matthew's clothes. There's always plenty of them."

Iris grabbed the nearest basket of laundry, her face scrunching as she lifted the pile of heavy, soiled clothes. "Grandma, seriously, this can't all be from one week. Did he roll around in the dirt for fun?"

"With his job in the orchard it's hard to keep clean." Wilma shook out a pair of Matthew's work pants before tossing them into the wash. "It's a man's job."

"I don't see why he can't do his own washing. He's a grown man. He can handle it."

"Well, I've always taken care of the house and the guests who come and go. It's the least I can do for him," Wilma replied, closing the lid on the washer.

"Why can't we just marry him off to Grace already so she can do it for him?" Iris grinned mischievously.

Wilma's eyes held a hint of sadness. "It's not that simple. Love doesn't always follow a straight line. Sometimes it takes a while for two people to figure out if they can walk the same path." They finished the washing in companionable silence, and once it was done, Wilma announced, "I think we should visit Cherish and your cousins at the dairy. But I'll need a rest first."

"I'd love that. I'll go for a walk in the orchard while you're resting."

"Don't get lost," Wilma called after her jokingly.

Iris headed toward the orchard and looked for Matthew. She couldn't see him anywhere and when she was heading back to the house, she found Matthew taking a burlap sack off the back of his cart. "Matthew, I need you to hitch the horse and buggy for us soon. I would do it myself, but... well, I don't exactly know how."

Matthew chuckled. "Still learning what we do around here, huh?"

"Something like that. I've got sewing covered, though, so at least I'm useful for something. I can cook as well."

"I don't mind helping."

They walked to the barn together, and Iris couldn't help asking, "So, Matthew, what's going on with you and Grace?"

Matthew's shoulders tensed. "Did someone ask you to ask me?"

"No. It just seems like everyone talks about it. Grandma said you've been dating her for the last ten years and still no marriage."

"Yeah, well, more like one year if you combine all the months and strike off the months we weren't talking. It's more complicated than people think."

As Matthew grabbed the tack from the wall, Iris leaned against the doorway. "Well, are you afraid of commitment? The rumors are that Grace's been waiting for you all this time."

"That's what everyone thinks, isn't it? That I'm the one dragging my feet?" He turned to face her. "I was ready to marry her. I told her that. But she's the one who changed her mind."

"Grace changed her mind?"

"Yep. She said she wasn't sure anymore, that she needed time to think. So I gave her time. But now it's been years, and nothing's changed. Okay, I should explain there were a few starts and stops. One of them might've been me who ended things, but mostly it was Grace."

"So what happened between you two? Why all the stops and starts?"

"I don't know. Maybe she realized I wasn't what she wanted after all."

"Maybe she got tired of waiting for you to propose in a romantic way."

Matthew's eyes met hers with a hard gaze. "Life's not always simple. Love can be complicated, and it's hardly ever romantic, whatever that is. You're too young to understand, Iris."

"Too young? I'm old enough to marry, so I think I'm old enough to understand that stringing someone along for ten years isn't fair. But you say that's not what happened so I'm sorry I thought that."

"Marrying and understanding love are two different things. You can marry someone without really knowing what it means to build a life with them."

"I get that it's complicated, but you're a middle-aged man living with your elderly aunt's best friend. Don't you think it's time to figure out what or who you really want?"

Matthew's expression softened. "I know it's time. I've known for a long time. Grace deserves better than someone who can't make up his mind, and I don't want to hurt her anymore. So, let it go."

"Then stop dragging this out. Talk to her. Either you're going to be together, or you're not. But this limbo... it's not fair to either of you."

"It's over for me, but maybe other people don't realize it. I will probably talk with her to make sure she's not thinking anything will come of us. Will that make you happy?"

"Yes, of course. I think you know what you need to do. You've just been scared to do it."

"I'll write her a letter."

"Good. Writing your feelings down is a good way because then you won't forget anything and you can word everything just right."

"If you say so."

He finished hitching the buggy, then looked over at her again. "Thanks for your help, Iris. I didn't know people were still talking about me and Grace."

"People always talk. If you ever need someone to talk with, I'm here. I'm not a kid anymore you know."

He grinned. "I know. You've grown up."

CHAPTER 7

HUNDREDS OF MILES AWAY, Grace folded another dress into her suitcase, smoothing out the fabric as she tried to focus on the task at hand. Her room was already half-packed, with clothing and books neatly arranged in piles on the floor. The wooden wardrobe next to her bed was nearly empty now, and the suitcase on her bed was slowly filling up.

Her adoptive mother, Leonie, sat on the edge of the bed, watching. "You've got most of your things packed already. You're not leaving for a couple of days."

"I know, but I want to have everything ready."

"Are you sure you don't need another suitcase?" Leonie asked.

Grace smiled faintly. "I'll only be gone for the summer, Ma. If I need anything else, I'm sure Christina or one of the others can lend it to me."

Leonie nodded, though the quiet concern in her eyes

remained. "It'll be strange not having you around. The house will feel a little emptier without you here."

Grace paused in her packing, looking up at her mother with a warm smile. "You've got plenty of children to keep you busy, Ma," she teased lightly.

Leonie chuckled, glancing toward the hallway where the faint sounds of her younger children playing could be heard. As the wife of a bishop and mother to a large family, Leonie's days were rarely quiet. Grace had always appreciated the warmth and love that filled their home, even with all the noise and chaos that came with it.

As Grace resumed packing, folding another dress and placing it into the suitcase, her mind wandered. She would get to know her birth mother more and if God willed it she would meet a suitable man.

"You've said nothing about Matthew. Are you certain you'll be all right with him being so close?"

Grace stiffened slightly, keeping her eyes on the clothes in her hands. "I'm not going to have anything to do with him. I'm done with all that back-and-forth. He's made his choice, and I've made mine."

"That's wise, but what are your plans for after summer. I suppose it depends what happens, is that right?"

"I was thinking... maybe even after the summer, I could stay on with Christina for a while. Our community is wonderful, but it's so small. If I want to find someone to build a life with, I need to broaden my horizons."

Leonie nodded in agreement. "Christina might be able to help you meet people. And I'm sure Wilma will be a good ally for you. She's quite straightforward, and I think if you tell her your intentions, she'll know how to help."

Grace shook her head quickly, her hands gripping the edge of her suitcase. "No, Ma. Not Wilma. Matthew is staying with her."

"Ah, of course."

"I didn't expect him to stay so long at Wilma's, but it seems he's settled there now," Grace said.

"How do you know for sure?"

"Cherish told me in a letter. Christina never tells me anything about him unless I ask. But Cherish tells me everything about everyone even without me asking."

Leonie smiled. "That explains why those letters from Cherish are always so thick."

Grace nodded, though her heart felt heavy with the thought that the years were escaping her. It was time for her to be more than just the bishop's adopted daughter. She needed to be someone's wife, and the sooner that happened the better.

Leonie's smile returned. "Christina is a good woman. She'll take care of you."

Grace bit her lip, considering her next words carefully. "I just don't want anyone thinking I'm going there because of Matthew. I'm moving forward, not looking back."

"Whatever happens, God is in control of your path," Leonie assured her. "People will always gossip. That's just what they do. Don't let it affect you."

The thought of being in the same community as Matthew unsettled her, even as she tried to convince herself she was ready for this. "I suppose it'll be good practice. If I can handle being around Matthew maybe I'm ready for anything."

Leonie stood up. "Just remember to stay focused on what you want, not on what you used to want. Leave the past in the past."

Grace smiled, grateful for her mother's words of encouragement. "I'll write to you often and let you know how things are going."

"I'd like that," Leonie said, pulling her into a tight hug. "But don't feel like you have to. This summer is for you, Grace. Take all the time you need and remember to enjoy yourself. Life doesn't need to be serious all the time. Have some fun."

As Grace embraced her mother, she felt a surge of gratitude for the life she'd been given. Leonie and Zachariah had taken her in when she was just a baby, and they'd loved her as their own. But now, it was time for her to step out from under their protective wings and find her own path. "I'll miss you, and everyone," Grace whispered.

Leonie pulled back and cupped her face gently. "We'll miss you too, but we know this is what you need to do."

Grace nodded, blinking away the sudden tears that pricked at the corners of her eyes. "I should finish packing. There's one more bag to fill."

Leonie nodded and stepped back, giving her space. "I'll let you finish. Just remember, Grace—God will make a way."

"I know."

Grace watched as her mother left the room, the sound of her footsteps fading down the hall. Alone now, she looked at the other suitcase. This summer would be different. It had to be.

CHAPTER 8

Wilma and Iris set off in the horse and buggy to Cherish's house so Iris could visit with her cousins.

The rhythmic clip-clop of the hooves was a pleasant sound for Iris. "I'm so pleased to be here, Grandma. I just can't put it into words."

Wilma glanced over at her. "I'm glad to have you here."

Iris stared out the window feeling good about everything. The brief sense of peace was shattered when she spotted a flash from behind the trees on the roadside.

Squinting, Iris leaned forward, narrowing her eyes at the figure crouched down in the bushes. A second flash followed.

"What's going on?" Iris muttered, craning her neck. And then she saw him. It was Chess. He was holding up his phone, snapping pictures.

"What is it?" Wilma asked.

Iris sat bolt upright, her annoyance rising in an instant. "Grandma, stop the horse."

Wilma raised an eyebrow. "What's the matter?"

"Just pull over, please," Iris insisted.

Wilma tugged on the reins, slowing the buggy to a stop at the side of the road. Iris jumped out, her hands balled into fists as she marched toward the bushes.

"Chess!" she yelled, glaring at him. "What are you doing?"

Chess stood up, a smug grin spreading across his face as he held up his phone. "Just documenting your stay with the Amish, sis. Thought you'd want some memories to look back on."

"Memories?" Iris scoffed, her hands on her hips. "Why don't you just go home and stop spying on me?"

Chess shrugged nonchalantly, taking another photo. "It's a free country. I can do whatever I want. And besides, this is great material for when I tell everyone how you're 'finding yourself' with the Amish." He said the last part in a mocking tone, complete with air quotes.

Iris's blood boiled. "Get your own life, Chess! Stop following me around like some kind of... I don't even know what! A stalker!"

Chess's grin didn't fade. If anything, it grew wider. "Why would I? All my friends are getting a good laugh watching what my crazy sister's doing this summer. It's all over social media. They think you've totally lost it. You should read some of the comments."

"That's it." Iris stepped forward, ready to snatch the phone out of his hand, but before she could make a move, Wilma's voice cut through the air.

"Iris!" Wilma's tone was firm but calm. "Get back in the buggy."

Iris froze, her chest heaving with frustration, her eyes still locked on her brother's smirk. For a moment, she wanted nothing more than to teach him a lesson, but Wilma's presence kept her in check.

"Calm down and ignore him," Wilma added.

Clenching her jaw, Iris took a deep breath, exhaling slowly as she forced herself to turn away from Chess. She knew being Amish meant turning the other cheek and she had to do all these things sooner or later. "Fine," she muttered under her breath, storming back to the buggy. She climbed in, sitting beside her grandmother without saying another word. Her hands trembled slightly as she tried to calm herself, the anger still simmering beneath the surface.

Chess's laughter echoed behind them as Wilma clicked the reins, and the horse and buggy started moving again.

Iris sat silently, staring at the road ahead, her emotions swirling. After a few moments of tense silence, she finally spoke, her voice quieter now. "I'm sorry, Grandma. I didn't mean to lose my temper like that. I just... I can't stand him sometimes."

Wilma glanced at her. "Family can bring out the best in us but sometimes the worst. Don't worry about it."

Iris sighed, slumping back in her seat. "I really thought I'd be getting away from him this summer. But it's like he's everywhere, always trying to make my life harder."

Wilma gave her a sympathetic look. "It's hard for him too, you know. He's at that age where he's trying to figure things out. But I do agree that following you around and causing trouble isn't helping anyone."

Iris bit her lip, hesitating before continuing. "You should see his friends. They're bad news, Grandma. Older boys, troublemakers. Mom and Dad aren't happy about it at all."

Wilma's eyebrows furrowed slightly. "What do you mean, troublemakers?"

"They're the kind of boys you see lurking around at the farmer's markets. You know, standing in groups, smoking, making rude comments at people who walk by. They've got that look, like they're always up to something. I don't know why Chess hangs out with them. Mom and Dad have been fighting with him about it for months."

Wilma's expression grew more serious. "I see. Well, that doesn't sound good. When you're growing up you have to be very careful who your friends are. And I suppose even when you're grown-up."

"I just don't understand why he's acting like this. He used to be annoying, sure, but now… now it's like he's trying to cause trouble on purpose. And those friends of his are making him worse."

Wilma was silent for a moment, guiding the buggy along the quiet country road. After a few moments, she spoke. "It sounds like Chess is trying to fit in with the wrong crowd. Maybe he feels lost, like he's not sure where he belongs."

"Yeah, well, that's no excuse for acting like a jerk," Iris muttered, folding her arms across her chest.

"No, it's not," Wilma agreed. "But it's also not something you can fix by getting angry. He's going to have to find his own way, Iris. Just like you're finding yours."

Iris looked down at her hands, her anger fading into something softer—something like sadness. "I just wish he'd stop making everything so hard for everyone. He needs to leave me alone and just worry about himself."

Wilma patted her hand gently. "He's still young. Give him time."

Iris nodded, though she wasn't entirely convinced. Chess seemed determined to make things difficult, and she wasn't sure how much more patience she had left.

CHAPTER 9

As the buggy rolled up the long driveway to Aunt Cherish's house, Iris noticed the stillness—no children, no barking dogs, just cows grazing in the field.

"Looks like everyone's out," Iris said, glancing at Wilma.

Wilma nodded. "Seems that way. But Cherish should be here." She tugged the reins gently, slowing the buggy in front of the large, white farmhouse.

Iris hopped down first, adjusting her apron, and Wilma followed more slowly, her hands smoothing her skirt as she approached the door. Before Iris could knock, the door swung open, and there stood Cherish, her face lighting up with a warm smile.

"Well, look who's here!" Cherish exclaimed, stepping forward to give Iris a hug. "You look lovely in those clothes, Iris."

Iris looked down at her dress and apron. "I made them myself, and Christina showed me how to make a prayer *kapp.*"

"Where is everyone?" Wilma asked Cherish.

"They're out right now. The children are over at Honor's place for the day. They're helping paint the barn. Malachi's in the dairy somewhere."

Suddenly, the upstairs window flew open, and Tabitha's head appeared. "I'm here, Mamm!" she declared, waving grandly.

Cherish sighed and looked upward. "Close the window and finish your room."

The window slammed shut, then reopened a second later. "Just so you know, I found three whole dust bunnies. And I'm naming them Dusty, Rusty, and Krusty."

Wilma and Iris laughed.

"Tabitha!" Cherish sighed as the window closed again. "She's in trouble."

"Again?" Wilma said with a smile.

Cherish nodded as they stepped into the house. "She has a gift for turning every chore into a huge production. Come inside."

In the kitchen, Cherish motioned for them to sit at the large oak table.

"I'll be here all summer, Aunt Cherish."

Cherish smiled. "Plenty of time for work and play."

Wilma raised an eyebrow. "Let's not forget why she's here. She's trying to see if she wants to join us."

Cherish leaned in. "I've got a little bit of gossip. Guess who's coming back for the summer?"

Loud footsteps thundered down the stairs, and Tabitha appeared like a whirlwind. "I'm done! I've tamed the wild dust bunnies and emerged without so much as a scratch." She ran and hugged her grandmother and then Iris.

Cherish folded her arms. "Have you really finished cleaning?"

Tabitha's eyes widened. "Of course! I'm the fastest cleaner in the county. I could clean the bishop's entire house in under an hour if I had to."

Wilma smiled and shook her head. "You're just like your mother was at your age."

Tabitha's face beamed. "See? Mammi gets it. Although, I'd need extra pay for the bishop's haus. He has so many stairs."

"No one is paying you to clean anything, especially around here. Are you really finished?" Cherish asked again.

"Of course. If you must know, I even organized my drawer of very important things. That took a while. I have a lot of inventions."

"Inventions?" Iris asked.

Tabitha nodded. "Yes. Like my sock puppet singers." She raised her hands, miming tiny singing puppets. "They sing hymns during boring chores. They're quite good."

"Tabitha, please sit down," Cherish said, fighting a smile.

Tabitha plopped into a chair. "Wait—Mamm, you said you had gossip, but you always tell us not to gossip." She waved her hand dismissively. "Forget I said that. Who's coming back?"

Cherish hesitated, then gave in. "It's Grace, Christina's daughter."

Tabitha's jaw dropped. "Grace? No way!" She turned to Iris, eyes gleaming. "She's so nice. She used to sneak me extra cookies. Well, she did when I was a kid. But I'm practically a teenager now."

"You're ten," Cherish reminded her.

"Ten and a half!" Tabitha corrected. "Basically a grown-up."

Wilma chuckled. "I don't know about that."

"I bet she's coming back to make Matthew fall in love with her again. It's like one of those novels, you know?" Tabitha said.

Cherish raised a finger at her daughter. "Let the adults talk. You can listen, but don't take over the conversation all the time. This is why your brothers call you Blabitha."

Tabitha's mouth fell open, then she slowly closed it.

Wilma felt a pang of sympathy for the girl but couldn't think of what to say. She looked at Iris instead. "Grace was adopted by Leonie and Bishop Zachariah. Zachariah is Malachi's uncle."

"Oh, I see. I knew that, but I think I forgot it."

Wilma asked Cherish, "Do you know how long she's staying?"

"In her letter, she said it's an extended stay." Cherish poured water into glasses and set them on the table. "I don't know why she bothers with Matthew after all this time."

Wilma and Iris exchanged looks, both remembering their conversation earlier. "We were just talking about Grace," Iris said, shaking her head in surprise. "That's… unexpected."

"Not really. She was bound to come back soon. Her mother's here after all," Cherish said. "Christina doesn't get to spend much time with her."

"We'll find out soon enough, I guess." Iris couldn't help but feel a strange sense of anticipation stirring inside her. Grace had been at the center of so much conversation today, and now she was coming back.

CHAPTER 10

AFTER LEAVING Cherish's house Wilma and Iris decided to visit with Ada.

Wilma drove the buggy, her hands loosely holding the reins. "Soon we'll get you some friends. Sorry that your cousins were out today."

Iris glanced at her grandmother, shaking her head with a gentle smile. "Tabitha was there."

"Oh yes. Tabitha."

"It's fine, really. I've got the whole summer to get to know people my age in the community. I'm sure I'll have plenty of chances to make friends at the Sunday meeting."

"I'm glad to hear that, Iris. You're always so positive." She guided the horse up the final stretch of the driveway leading to Ada's.

They visited briefly with Ada, leaving behind a basket of food and making sure everything was in order before heading back to the orchard. By the time they returned home, the cool evening air had settled in giving much needed relief from the day's heat.

As she was getting out of the buggy, Iris spotted movement on the porch. There, kneeling by the steps, was Matthew, hammering in nails with a focused expression. The soft clinking of metal against wood echoed in the stillness.

"Matthew's fixing things?" Wilma said, surprised. "I wasn't expecting him to work on the porch today."

Iris leaned forward, watching as Matthew stood up and wiped his brow with the back of his hand. He looked up and smiled when he saw them approaching.

Then he walked over to them. "It took me a bit longer than I'd planned, but I needed the proper nails to get the job done. It took some searching, but I got it all sorted."

Wilma raised an eyebrow, clearly impressed but still processing the fact that Matthew had taken care of the repairs without being nagged. Perhaps he was making an effort for the sake of their visitor. "You fixed the porch?"

Matthew nodded. "Not just the porch. I also fixed the stuck window in the living room and the leaking tap outside." He glanced over at Iris before he looked back at Wilma.

"Oh, thank you, Matthew. Well done."

Matthew's smile widened, clearly pleased with her compliment. "I'm just glad I could help out."

"You've been busy today," Wilma said.

Matthew shrugged modestly. "It's no trouble. Just things that needed to be done." He quickly made his way over to the buggy and started unhitching the horse. "I'll take care of this for you," he called over his shoulder.

Wilma smiled. "I appreciate it."

As Matthew worked to unhitch the buggy, Iris stepped onto the newly repaired porch, running her hand along the smooth wood. It was solid and sturdy—just like Matthew. She glanced over at him.

"Well, I guess we've got a few less things to worry about around here," Wilma said.

Iris smiled, glancing at her grandmother. "Yes, thanks to Matthew."

Wilma nodded slowly, her eyes drifting to Matthew as he finished with the buggy and began leading the horse to the stable. There was a lingering silence between them as they both stood watching him.

As Matthew led the horse toward the barn, he paused, looking up at Iris. "Hey, Iris, do you want to learn how to feed and care for the horses?"

CHAPTER 11

IRIS BLINKED, momentarily surprised by Matthew's offer. She glanced at her grandmother, unsure if she should accept, but Wilma gave her a nod of encouragement.

"Sure, I'd like to learn," she called back, and with a burst of energy, she hurried over to the barn where Matthew was waiting.

"First thing you need to know," Matthew began, "is how to unhitch the buggy properly. I'll show you that tomorrow. You don't want to leave anything tangled or in a mess. You always want to leave everything neat and that way you'll know where to find everything. A place for everything and everything in it's place." He led the horse into a stable.

"I'm a little afraid of horses."

"Nah, you don't need to be."

"They're so big," Iris said. "I guess it's because I haven't really grown up with them. We never had any horses of our own.'

"Be nice to them and don't show fear or hesitation around them. If you do, they'll get nervous. If you're normal, you won't have a problem."

"Okay. I'll remember that."

Matthew showed Iris how to prepare the feed, carefully measuring it out and pouring it into the trough. "You want to make sure they get the right amount."

Iris leaned in closer than she needed to. "You make it look so easy."

Matthew nodded, focused on the task. "It's not hard once you get the hang of it."

As Iris finished feeding, she tucked a loose strand of hair behind her ear. "Though I suppose if I had someone like you around, I wouldn't need to learn all this."

Matthew glanced at her. "Every horse owner should know the basics. Can't always count on having help."

"No, I guess not." Iris let her hand brush against his as she replaced the feed scoop. "But it's nice having you teach me."

Matthew paused, studying her for a moment with a hint of a smile. "You're a quick learner. Won't need my help for long."

Iris's cheeks warmed under his gaze. "Maybe I just like having you around."

Matthew turned back to the horse. "You should go inside before your grandmother comes looking for you. I'll be there soon."

Iris watched him for a moment longer, fighting disappointment. "Okay." She'd always had a crush on Matthew and he'd admitted he wasn't going to marry Grace. "I just want to know one thing."

He looked over at her. "What's that?"

"What do you think about me? Be honest."

He shrugged. "You're determined, you're not afraid to get your hands dirty, and you've got a good head on your shoulders. Not every girl in town would be out here helping with the horses. With your parents having so much money, you could have anything you want—be anywhere you want. You chose to be here, and that shows what's important to you."

Iris's heart flooded with gladness. His approval of her meant everything. "I've wanted to be here for as long as I can remember and now Obadiah has gone, I can be with Grandma and help."

Matthew's smile softened. "You're very kind, Iris. She's excited to have you here."

Iris's expression faltered for a moment, and she looked away. "I just want to make sure she's taken care of. She's done so much for everyone, and I want to repay that in whatever way I can."

Matthew's gaze lingered on her for a moment before he nodded. "She's happier than I've seen her in ages. So, do you think you'll stay here after the summer?" Matthew asked.

Iris tilted her head, considering the question. "Oh yes. I love it here . It's peaceful, and it feels... right."

Matthew nodded thoughtfully. "There's a lot of good in this community. It's not always easy, but it's home. Even though I didn't grow up here, I prefer it."

Iris smiled softly. "Yeah, I can see that."

Matthew leaned against the stall, crossing his arms as he looked at Iris. "I think you've got a knack for this and there's no need to be nervous around the horses. All Wilma's horses have got good natures. They're all the ones Levi bred and he knew a lot about horses. You did well today."

Iris laughed. "I think you're just being nice, but thanks. I'm learning."

Matthew grinned. "You'll be an expert in no time. And, who knows? Maybe you won't need a man around after all because you'll know how everything's done."

Iris raised an eyebrow. "Oh, I don't know about that. I kind of like the idea of having someone around to help with the heavy lifting."

Matthew chuckled. "In time, I'm sure there'll be plenty of men willing to help you, Iris."

She knew what he meant by 'in time'—that she was too young right now.

There was a brief pause as their eyes met, a shared moment of understanding passing between them before Matthew broke the silence with a playful smile. "But until then, I'll keep showing you the ropes."

Iris smiled, feeling a little lighter. "Deal."

"We're finished here. Let's go," Matthew said.

Together they headed back to the house.

CHAPTER 12

THE FOLLOWING MORNING, Iris and Wilma set out for a walk through the apple orchard. Matthew was already working among the trees. The orchard stretched out before them, row upon row of apple trees, their branches heavy with the promise of fruit to come.

Wilma smiled as she looked around. "I think we're in for another good harvest this year."

"Oh goody. I love harvest time. It's so much fun."

Wilma nodded. "And a lot of hard work."

Iris breathed in deeply. "I know how Mom loves the apple trees so much, but I don't. Not really. Does she think I'm going to take over looking after her orchard and this one?"

"I'm not sure. You'll have to ask her, but that's too far into the future to worry about."

The gentle rustling of leaves and the occasional call of birds filled the air, and Iris couldn't help but feel a sense of peace among the trees.

"I love walking through here," Wilma said after a while, her voice soft, almost as if she were talking to herself. "It reminds me of all the people who have been part of this orchard. Your grandfather, my first husband, worked hard to plant the first rows here. He had such a vision for this place. He wanted to leave something lasting for the family."

"A legacy," Iris suggested.

"That's right."

Iris glanced at her grandmother, noticing the distant look in her eyes. "It must be comforting, having all these memories here. It's like they're all still with you in a way."

Wilma nodded. "Yes, it is. This orchard is a part of all of them. Obadiah had a special touch with the trees - he could spend hours perfecting each branch through careful pruning."

"What about Levi your second husband?"

Wilma smiled. "He tried working in the orchard, but he stepped back after a while. It wasn't for him. It caused all kinds of problems, but then your mother stepped back in to take over. Then she had you, and then Chess—"

"Let's not talk about him while I'm here, okay?" Iris suggested.

Wilma laughed. "Okay."

While they walked, Iris found herself feeling a little braver. "Grandmother," she began hesitantly, "I hope this isn't too delicate of a question, but... I've been thinking about it for a while. Did you... did you love each of your husbands the same?"

Wilma slowed her pace and turned to look at Iris, a thoughtful expression crossing her face. "That's not an easy question, Iris, but it's a good one."

Iris felt her cheeks flush with embarrassment, but she

pressed on. "I mean, is it possible to love three people? Three men? I've wondered about it, and I didn't know if—well, if you felt the same about each of them."

Wilma didn't answer right away. She seemed to be considering the question carefully, her gaze drifting out over the rows of apple trees. After a long moment, she spoke. "Each one touched my heart in his own way. Your grandfather was my first love - young, exciting, full of dreams we built together. Levi brought peace after loss, a steady warmth that made me feel secure. And Obadiah... he opened my mind to new perspectives, always encouraging deeper thought and understanding."

Iris nodded, absorbing her grandmother's words. "I only really remember Obadiah, she admitted after a moment. "He was a lovely man. He was always kind to me, even when I was a little terror running through the orchard and hanging around."

Wilma chuckled softly. "Yes, he was a good man. He had a lot of patience, especially with you and your cousins."

They walked in silence for a few more moments. "Last night, Matthew said that Levi bred all your horses and that's why they are so calm and good."

Wilma nodded. "That's right. He loved his horses. That was his passion, just as your grandfather Josiah had his calling with the apple trees."

"So your first and second husbands had a lot of passion."

Wilma giggled. "I suppose you could say that. They were devoted to their interests."

Finally, Iris worked up the nerve to ask another question that had been on her mind. "Would you ever marry again?"

Wilma threw her head back and laughed. "Oh, goodness, no. I'm far too old for that, Iris. I've had my time, and I've been blessed with three wonderful marriages. That chapter of my life is complete."

Iris wasn't sure why she'd been nervous about asking, but now it seemed so obvious. Of course, Wilma wouldn't remarry. She had lived a full life already.

Iris then noticed that they were nearing the fence line that divided Wilma's orchard from the neighboring property—her family's property. Her stomach sank a little when she realized where they were.

"Let's go the other way," Iris said quickly, stopping in her tracks. "I don't want to risk seeing my brother. It would totally ruin the rest of my day."

Wilma smiled. "He's hardly ever outside, is he?"

Iris rolled her eyes. "Exactly. He's probably inside playing video games or hanging out with his stupid friends. But I'd rather avoid him altogether."

Wilma chuckled softly, turning to follow Iris's lead as they changed direction. "You know, you can't stay away from him forever."

"I can certainly try," Iris muttered under her breath.

CHAPTER 13

IRIS AND WILMA continued their walk. Up ahead, Matthew moved between the trees. He was thinning the apples—a tedious but necessary job to ensure the best fruit would thrive.

Iris found herself slowing down, watching the way he worked. He had his sleeves rolled up, revealing tanned forearms as his hands moved with quiet confidence through the branches. There was something mesmerizing about how gentle those work-roughened hands could be.

"He's really dedicated, isn't he?" Iris said. "I mean, he's been fixing everything at the house, and now it's great to see him working like this."

Wilma smiled. "That's the way of all Amish men, Iris. You'll find that out. Hard work is part of their nature, part of our faith. Matthew is no different from the rest in that regard."

Iris nodded thoughtfully, her gaze still following Matthew as he moved from tree to tree. "I guess that makes sense." Then, after a moment of hesitation, she added, "Do you think anyone's told him Grace is coming back?"

Wilma paused, her eyes narrowing slightly as she considered the question. "I wonder. I can't imagine he wouldn't have heard by now, but it's possible no one's mentioned it. We didn't."

Iris shrugged. "He hasn't said anything to me about it, if he does know. You'd think he'd at least mention it."

"Well, let's continue to keep it to ourselves for now. There's no need to stir things up unnecessarily."

"Okay," Iris agreed, glancing at her grandmother with a nod. She could sense there was more to the situation than Wilma was letting on, but she didn't push it. If Wilma thought it was best to keep quiet, Iris would follow her lead.

They continued walking in comfortable silence for a while longer, and as they neared the house, Wilma turned to Iris. "You know, maybe we should take Ada out for the day. It'd be nice to get her out of the house for a bit. We could visit Christina and see if we can find out what's going on with Grace."

Iris chuckled, the idea of finding out more about Grace suddenly felt like a fun adventure. "That sounds like a good plan. And I can see the twins! It's been ages since I've visited them."

Wilma laughed, clearly pleased by Iris's enthusiasm. "Oh, they'd love that. They've always adored you. But don't go offering to make everyone dresses. You don't want to spend your entire summer on your sewing machine."

"Why not? I like sewing. I could make them some cute little dresses. It wouldn't take long."

Wilma shook her head. "All I'm saying is pace yourself. The summer will be gone before you know it."

Iris was already imagining the twins in the dresses she would make them. "Okay, I'll just do one at a time. Actually, remind me to have Matthew move my sewing machine closer to the window. I could use the extra light."

"It's probably not the best idea to rely on me for reminders. I've been so forgetful lately. I'll probably forget this entire conversation."

"Fair enough. I'll make a mental note of it myself."

Iris couldn't help but feel a sense of contentment settle over her. The orchard, the house, her grandmother—it all felt like home in just the way she thought it would.

"Let's get ready," Wilma said, breaking the peaceful silence as they neared the porch. "I'm sure Ada will be thrilled to get out for a bit. She hasn't had much excitement lately."

CHAPTER 14

WITH ADA comfortably settled in the buggy, Wilma and Iris made their way to Christina's house. The conversation between them had been light, mostly filled with easy chatter, but there had been one agreement during the ride: they wouldn't mention Grace unless Christina brought it up first. None of them wanted to stir anything unnecessarily.

When they arrived, the familiar farmhouse came into view, its wide porch framed by colorful flowers. As they climbed the steps, Iris felt a flutter of excitement at seeing the twins again. They always brought so much energy with them.

Wilma knocked on the door, and from inside, they could hear the unmistakable sound of running feet. Moments later, the door flew open, and one of the twins, Olivia let out an excited squeal. *"Mamm,* visitors," she called over her shoulder. "Mamm, Wilma's here with Ada. And Iris too."

From somewhere deeper in the house, Christina's voice rang out, "Olivia, stop yelling in the house. How many times have I told you—" The scolding cut off as Christina rounded the corner from the kitchen, her expression shifting immediately when she saw her guests. Christina hurried forward to greet them, wiping her hands on her apron as she ushered them into the cozy living room. "I wasn't expecting company, but it's a lovely surprise. Please, sit down. Look at you, Iris. You look lovely in those clothes."

"Denke," Iris said, practicing her new words. "And the prayer kapp you helped me with."

"It looks lovely."

They all took their seats, and no sooner had Iris settled into her chair than the twins pounced. "Iris, how do you like it here so far?" Olivia asked excitedly, her eyes wide with curiosity.

"Are you going to be staying the whole summer?" Anna asked.

"Where are you living now?" Olivia chimed in again, clearly not finished with her questions. "Will you live with *Mammi* the whole time? Or are you getting your own place?"

Iris laughed, feeling slightly overwhelmed but amused by the rapid-fire questions. "One question at a time," she said, holding up her hands playfully. "I love it here so far. I'm staying with Grandma, and I'll be here for the whole summer, so you'll probably get tired of me soon enough."

The twins shook their heads furiously, both exclaiming at once, "No, we won't."

Christina laughed from her place on the couch. "All right, girls, let's give Iris a chance to breathe. Anna, why don't you make us some tea?"

Before Anna could answer, Olivia piped up. "I'll go too!" she said, jumping to her feet.

Christina raised an eyebrow but didn't seem surprised. "Of course you will," she said with a fond smile. "Those two do everything together these days," she explained to Iris. "They even insist on wearing the same clothes. Can't get them to dress differently if you tried."

Iris smiled, filing that bit of information away in the back of her mind. She would love to sew them matching dresses and started daydreaming about the fabrics she'd use.

"I have some exciting news. Grace is coming back for the whole of the summer. She'll be here in a couple of days," Christina said.

The twins, who had returned from the kitchen with a tray of tea, let out excited squeals at the news. "Grace's coming back?" Anna asked.

"Yes." Christina nodded.

Iris smiled, taking the teacup that Anna handed her. "That's wonderful."

Ada, who had been quiet up until that point, tilted her head curiously and asked the question on everyone's mind. "Is she going to try again with Matthew?"

Christina's expression shifted slightly, though she didn't seem surprised by the question. "No, definitely not," she said firmly. "Grace's only coming back to see me and the girls. And, of course, Mark. She's not here for Matthew."

There was a subtle pause in the room, as if everyone was processing the weight of Christina's words. Iris glanced at Wilma, who seemed content to let the conversation play out without adding anything more.

The twins, oblivious to the tension, were too excited about Grace's return to care much about the details. "We can't wait to see her," Olivia said, practically bouncing with excitement. "We'll show her all the new things around town and our lambs."

Iris couldn't help but wonder how it would affect Matthew—and whether Christina was as certain as she seemed that Grace wasn't coming back for him.

CHAPTER 15

As the afternoon wore on, Iris, Wilma, and Ada climbed back into the buggy and headed toward Ada's house. They had just turned onto a narrow stretch of road when, out of nowhere, the sound of a car engine roaring broke the peaceful countryside calm. A sleek, dark vehicle came speeding toward them, its horn blaring loudly. Wilma's grip on the reins tightened, and the horse gave an anxious whinny, shifting restlessly beneath the harness as the car wooshed past them heading in the opposite direction.

"Whoa, easy now," Wilma murmured, expertly calming the horse with soft words. "It's all right."

Iris, her heart racing from the sudden noise, turned her head to watch the car speed away down the road. Her stomach twisted with an uneasy feeling as she caught a glimpse of the driver. "That's Chess," she said, her voice rising slightly in surprise. "He's driving one of Dad's cars."

Wilma's eyes flicked toward the retreating car, her brow furrowed with concern. "Chess? Driving?"

Before Iris could respond, the unmistakable wail of a police siren echoed through the air. A police car, lights flashing and siren blaring, zoomed past them, heading in the same direction as the car that had just passed.

Iris's breath caught in her throat, and she turned to Wilma, her eyes wide. "The police are chasing him."

"He's not old enough to drive, surely, is he?" Ada asked.

Wilma shook her head slowly, her expression serious. "No, he's not. He's far too young to be driving on his own."

"Dad will be furious, and Mom too."

Ada made a gentle suggestion. "Maybe the police are chasing someone else."

Wilma glanced at Iris. "Do you want me to turn around?"

"No. He was going too fast. He could be anywhere by now." Iris felt a knot of worry forming in her chest. She knew Chess could be reckless—he had always been a bit of a wild card, especially when it came to following rules—but taking their dad's car without permission was a whole new level of irresponsibility.

Wilma kept her focus on the horse, making sure the animal remained calm and steady after the sudden disturbances. "If it was Chess, we'll find out soon enough."

The familiar sight of Ada's house came into view, and Wilma pulled the buggy to a stop in front of the small farmhouse. Ada, who had been sitting quietly during the ride, gave Wilma a grateful smile as she prepared to get down from the buggy.

"Thank you for the lovely and eventful day, Wilma. Keep me updated about Chess," Ada said.

Iris forced a smile, though her thoughts were still tangled up in the events that had just unfolded. After walking Ada to her door, she climbed back into the buggy.

"Let's get home," Wilma said quietly as they started back.

As they started the journey to Wilma's house, Iris couldn't stop thinking about what had just happened. "Do you think we should tell Dad?" she asked after a while.

Wilma pursed her lips, clearly deep in thought. "I'm not sure yet," she admitted. "We don't even know for certain if it was Chess driving, and we don't want to jump to conclusions. Are you sure it was your father's car?"

"Yes. It was the same plate number. I didn't think he'd do something like this."

Wilma gave a small sigh. "Boys that age... they sometimes don't think things through. Especially when they're trying to prove something to themselves or others."

"I just worry about the police and all."

Wilma nodded. "Well, if they stopped him traveling at that speed, they might've helped prevent him getting into an accident and hurting himself or someone else."

"That's true."

As Wilma and Iris pulled into the driveway, Iris's stomach sank. Carter's car—the same one they had seen speeding past earlier—was rammed into the little building that had once served as a shop in front of Wilma's house. Half the structure was gone, and the car lay buried under a heap of rubble.

CHAPTER 16

The once-sturdy structure was now half-demolished, wood splintered and debris scattered across the gravel. The car was wedged into the side of the building, its front crumpled, the hood smoking faintly. Two police officers were taking photos and talking to each other in low, serious voices.

Iris gasped, her hand flying to her mouth as the buggy came to a halt. "Oh no... what happened?"

Wilma's face had gone pale. "I'm not sure."

Iris jumped down from the buggy and ran toward her father's car, her heart pounding in her chest. What if something had happened to Chess? She couldn't see him anywhere. As she approached, she saw her mother and father standing together, their faces etched with worry and frustration.

"Where's Chess?" Iris called out to them.

Carter, his face grim, turned to her with a heavy sigh. "Chess and his friends are being held at the police station."

Iris froze, her breath catching in her throat. "What happened?"

Carter rubbed the back of his neck, glancing toward the wrecked car with a pained expression. "Some of his friends stole money from a store, and they were using my car to escape. The police were chasing them, and Chess lost control. He crashed as you can see."

Iris felt like the ground had been pulled out from under her. Chess? Stealing? She had known her brother was reckless, but this… this was beyond anything she could have imagined. Her head spun and she felt weak all over.

Florence, her arms crossed tightly over her chest, spoke up. "The police are interviewing everyone involved. Chess is being held at the station for now, and we've decided we're going to leave him there longer than he needs to be. Maybe a night in a cell will knock some sense into him."

Wilma caught up to Iris, but had heard most of what they'd said. "Has he been arrested?"

Carter shook his head. "Not officially. I called my lawyer and in this county for minors, the police will hold them temporarily if they're involved in a crime. He hasn't been formally charged yet, but they're keeping him for questioning."

Iris felt her head swimming, a mixture of shock, disbelief, and embarrassment flooding her senses. "I can't believe this," she whispered, holding her head in her hands. "I'm embarrassed to even call him my brother."

Florence shot her a sharp glare, her eyes narrowing. "I know you're upset, but he's your brother, and he's in real trouble. This isn't just about embarrassment—it's about what happens to him next."

Iris bristled at the tone, but before she could say anything in response, she felt the familiar weight of Wilma's hand on her shoulder, offering a quiet, calming presence.

"I didn't mean it like that," Iris mumbled, her cheeks flushing with guilt. "It's just... I don't understand how he could do something like this."

"We're all trying to understand it," Carter said. "Chess has always been a bit wild, but this... this is a new low. He's in serious trouble now."

There was a long pause, the air thick with tension. The sound of the police officers taking photos and talking quietly in the background seemed distant, like something happening in a different world.

"Can I bring Romeo to Grandma's now?" Iris asked.

Florence's eyes widened in disbelief. "Your brother has crashed our car, he's in trouble with the law, and you're thinking about your cat?"

Iris winced at the sharpness in her mother's voice. "I—well, I just thought..." she stammered, realizing how absurd it sounded now that she had said it aloud.

Florence shook her head, letting out a frustrated sigh. "Unbelievable," she muttered under her breath.

Wilma spoke up. "Let's not be too hard on Iris. We're all a little shocked and Iris just misses her cat."

Iris nodded. "I do."

"I know," Wilma said.

Florence pressed her lips together, clearly still irritated, but she didn't say anything further. Instead, she turned back toward the wreckage.

"I'm sorry about this mess, Wilma. We'll handle all the repairs and have it back as good as new," Carter told her.

Wilma looked back at the shop that held many memories. "Well, don't worry too much. We could just demolish it."

"Nonsense, Wilma. We'll fix it," Florence insisted. "Dat built that nearly all by himself. I remember watching him do it. Mark and Earl helped as well."

"You're right. I was just trying to save money, and save everyone from more worry about things."

"Don't concern yourself with that. Chess has made this mess, and he'll have to pay it off in some way. He's not going to get off this lightly," Carter assured everyone.

"Good," Iris blurted out.

Carter put a hand on Florence's shoulder, offering a silent reassurance before turning back to Iris and Wilma. "We'll get through this. Chess has made a mess of things, and there'll be consequences for him. We just have to hope he learns from it."

Iris nodded numbly, feeling the weight of her father's words. She couldn't shake the image of Chess sitting in a police station, surrounded by people he shouldn't have been involved with in the first place. How had it all spiraled so far out of control?

All Iris could think of was that it served him right. This is what he deserved, but then there was a little piece of her that felt sorry for him even though he was the most annoying brother anyone ever had.

A SUMMER OF DISCOVERY

CHESS SAT IN THE SMALL, stark room of the police department, his knee bouncing up and down with nervous energy. The fluorescent lights buzzed overhead, and the dull gray walls seemed to close in around him. He was doing his best to keep calm, but the thought of being arrested made his heart race. He cleared his throat, leaning forward as he eyed the officers moving about behind the glass.

"You know who my dad is, right?" Chess blurted out suddenly, his voice louder than intended.

The officer at the desk raised an eyebrow but didn't respond right away.

Chess pressed on, trying to hide the panic creeping into his voice. "He's Carter Braithwaite. He's a billionaire. That's right. I didn't say millionaire, he's a billionaire… with a B. He started with online games and—he blew up. Not literally, I mean, he didn't blow anything up or anything like that," Chess stammered, realizing how ridiculous he sounded. "But his business, it blew up, you know? Like, huge. Am I… am I going to jail? My dad can bail me out, so let's not bother with all that."

The officers barely looked impressed. One of them walked over and looked at him directly. "You say your dad's got a lot of money?"

"That's right." Chess nodded eagerly.

"You're not trying to bribe us are you, son?"

Bribing? That had to be bad from how he said it. "No. No. I would never…" his voice trailed off as the officer turned and went back to his desk.

They treated Chess just like they would any other kid in trouble, but he wasn't just anyone. His father was Carter

Braithwaite. He always got special treatment when he mentioned who his dad was.

One of them, a tall, no-nonsense woman with a badge that read Officer Daniels, came over to where Chess sat. "We don't care who your father is, kid. Right now, you're here because you made some bad decisions, and that's what matters. You're not going to jail just yet, but we're going to have to ask you some questions. And until we get everything sorted you're better off keeping your mouth shut." She stared at Chess until he nodded.

"Okay." Chess had always thought his father would fix everything.

After a few minutes of formalities, Chess was led through the hallway toward the cells. His palms felt clammy as he followed the officer, his bravado crumbling with each step.

When they reached the holding area, the officer unlocked the door to the small, dimly lit cell where his friends were. They were lounging around, trying to look tough, throwing satisfied smiles and smart remarks like they didn't have a care in the world.

"Hey, about time you got here," one of them sneered, his arms crossed as he leaned against the wall.

Chess tried to muster up the same bravado, but all he could think about was how everything had spiraled out of control. How long would it take for all of them to realize just how much trouble they were in.

None of his friends seemed concerned. They'd all been here before they'd told him, so Chess had no choice but to act like he didn't care either.

CHAPTER 17

ONE OF CHESS'S FRIENDS, Tommy, sat up straighter on the long bench and smirked, glancing around at the others with a kind of arrogant ease. "Relax, Chess. You look worried. They won't do anything to us 'cause we're minors. Worst case, they'll send us to juvie, but not if it's your first time gettin' in trouble."

Chess swallowed hard. "Juvie?" Chess echoed, his voice cracking slightly. "That doesn't exactly sound like nothing."

Tommy shrugged. "It's not as bad as people make out. Do they know who your dad is?"

"Yeah. They don't care. I think it made them dislike me more when I told them."

Another boy, Darren, nodded in agreement, though his bravado didn't seem as solid as Tommy's. "Yeah, it's not like we were packing guns or robbing a bank. We just took some cash from that store. No big deal."

"No big deal?" Chess's stomach churned. He could hardly believe how casual his friends were being about the whole thing. "The police were chasing us. That doesn't happen for 'no big deal.' My dad's car is smashed and my grandmother's building is all wrecked," he muttered, glancing nervously toward the door of the cell.

Tommy laughed, though the sound felt hollow in the small, cramped space. "They just want to scare us, man. Trust me, with your dad being who he is, you'll get out of here faster than the rest of us."

Chess shifted uncomfortably at Tommy's comment, the weight of his father's name suddenly feeling heavy on his shoulders. "I don't think my dad will get me out of this," he said quietly, almost to himself. The realization that his father's influence couldn't shield him from his actions was starting to sink in.

Tommy waved a hand dismissively as he repeated, "You'll see that it's no big deal. No one's going to jail for this."

But even as Tommy tried to maintain his tough-guy act, Chess saw that the police hadn't treated this like a minor prank—they were serious. And the fact that they were sitting in a holding cell, waiting for their fates to be decided, made it painfully clear that this wasn't 'no big deal.'

CHAPTER 18

BACK AT WILMA'S HOUSE, Florence, Carter, and Wilma gathered in the living room, settling into a serious discussion about Chess's situation. Florence sighed, glancing at Carter, who gently held their daughter's hand.

"I'm sorry I snapped at you before, Iris. I'm just so upset and I didn't mean to take it out on you… about Romeo."

Iris nodded. "I know. It's okay."

"What are we going to do about Chess? He's too impulsive," Florence said softly.

Wilma nodded, her face creased with concern. "I think leaving him in the police station for a while might help him learn some responsibility."

"We'll definitely do that," Carter agreed. "I can't believe it's come to this. No one else in our family has ever been in trouble with the law."

Iris, sitting off to the side, felt a surge of frustration. The attention always seemed to be on Chess, and she thought being here would give her some space from that. Rising abruptly, she muttered something about needing air and stepped outside, ignoring her family's concerned looks.

The air outside was fresh but couldn't calm the frustration brewing inside her. She kicked at the dirt, pacing back and forth, trying to shake the weight of her family's endless attention on her brother.

Then she saw Matthew approaching. His presence alone unlocked a flood of emotion she couldn't contain. Without thinking, she ran toward him, tears streaming down her face. As she reached him, she flung herself into his arms, sobbing against his chest.

Matthew wrapped his strong arms around her, holding her close. "What's happened? Is Wilma okay?"

"She's okay." Iris pulled back slightly, pointing toward the shop where the car was still lodged halfway through the building. "Chess… he crashed into the shop, that old building at the front of the house. That's why he's at the police station right now. It's all so terrible and embarrassing. He was driving dad's car as a getaway for his friends after they stole money. The police chased them and he crashed."

Matthew's eyes widened. "Oh, I'm so sorry, Iris. That was the loud bang I heard earlier. I wondered what that was."

"Mom and Dad are in the house talking to Grandma about what to do with him."

CHAPTER 19

Chess sat alone in the cell, his back against the cold concrete wall, arms wrapped around his knees. The bravado that had carried him through the first few hours had crumbled away, leaving only a gnawing sense of dread.

One by one, his friends had been picked up by their parents. Tommy had been the first to leave, swaggering out of the cell with a wink and a grin as if it were all just another joke. Darren had followed not long after, his parents arriving with tight-lipped expressions. Each time the cell door had opened, Chess's heart had leapt, hoping his father would be next.

But hours passed, and the police station grew quieter. His foot tapped nervously against the floor, and he glanced at the door every few minutes, willing it to open. Finally, after night turned into morning, the door opened.

His father appeared in the doorway with a police officer. It had been a cold and uncomfortable night and the officers had refused his requests for a blanket.

Relief washed over Chess when he saw that his mother wasn't there too. His dad was always easier to deal with, less emotional, more practical. But even as he stood up to leave, he could feel the tension in the air. After an initial glance, his father didn't look at him again.

The officer gestured for Chess to follow. "Let's get you checked out," he said, his voice professional but not unkind. His dad still didn't say a word as they went through the formalities—signing paperwork, confirming Chess's identity. The police officer spoke with his dad briefly, outlining the next steps. Chess only caught bits and pieces—"possible juvenile charges," "formal warning," "dependent on investigation"—but none of it sounded good. Finally, after what seemed like forever, he was free to leave.

The ride home was tense. Chess sat in the passenger seat of one of his father's other cars, not the sleek black car he'd crashed. He wasn't brave enough to ask about how much damage there was. It looked pretty banged up when he and his friends tumbled out of it.

His hands clenched into fists in his lap. He tried not to look at his dad, but the disapproval hanging in the air was suffocating.

"I'm sorry, Dad," Chess said after a while.

Carter kept his eyes on the road. "I think more than words are needed. Although you can apologize to your grandmother. Why did you crash into her shop?"

"I didn't mean to," Chess mumbled, his face flushing with shame. "The cops were gaining on us, and I thought... I thought if I quickly turned into her driveway and parked behind something, they wouldn't find me. I was planning to hide the car behind the shop, but I heard the sirens and got distracted and then one of my friends yelled out turn, turn, so I turned too soon."

Carter shook his head, his jaw clenched. "So, in trying to hide from the police, you lead them to your grandmother's house so she can witness everything? She doesn't need to be involved in your antics."

"I didn't think," Chess blurted out. "I panicked."

"That much is obvious." Carter's voice was steely, his grip tightening on the steering wheel. "My car is damaged. And insurance won't pay for that either considering you're under age and should not have been behind the wheel."

Chess swallowed hard, trying to shrug off the seriousness of it all. "Yeah, but you've got loads of cars, and heaps of money so it doesn't really matter. You can afford to get it fixed."

But his dad wasn't smiling. He stared straight ahead, his expression grim. "Well, the thing is it's my money and not yours. You are going to rebuild your grandmother's building inch by inch with your own hands," he said, his tone final. "Even if it takes you a year to do it."

"What?"

"You heard me."

Chess huffed, thinking about how his friends would continue having fun without him. "Can't I just have the summer off before I start?"

"No."

Chess whipped his head toward his father, eyes wide in disbelief. "I'm just a kid. How am I supposed to fix a whole building?"

"You can figure it out. Then you can pay me back for the damage to the car."

"I'm not even old enough to have a job. Where will I get the money?"

"There's loads of things you can do. Mow lawns, odd jobs, get a paper route. I think it'll do you some good."

"But dad, I'm too young to do all those things. Mow lawns? Out in the sun with all that UV rays and stuff? It's not good for you. And who reads papers these days? It's all online. As for odd jobs, that's what poor people do, and if I have to remind you, I'm just a kid."

Carter's eyes finally flicked over to Chess, and there was no softness in them. "A kid?" he repeated, his voice filled with a quiet fury. "You weren't too young to get in my car and take it for a drive. You weren't too young to participate in a crime. And… there's no shame in doing any kind of work, no matter what it is."

Chess opened his mouth to protest but then quickly shut it, realizing he had nothing good to say. After a long pause, he muttered, "Yeah, but I didn't do the crime. I just drove the guys who did it."

Carter shook his head, his disappointment clear. "It makes no difference. You were just as much a part of the crime as if you'd been the one stealing the money. Can't you see that? You helped them get away, and now there are consequences for that."

His father's words cut deep, and for the first time, the gravity of the situation really started to sink in. Chess slumped down in his seat, staring at the floor. "Sorry, Dad."

Carter gave him a sidelong glance. "Your mother is heartbroken. Do you understand that? No one in our family has ever been in trouble with the law. You've dragged our name through the mud, and for what? To impress a bunch of kids who don't care about you?"

Chess swallowed the lump in his throat. He didn't have an answer to that. His friends—Tommy, Darren, and the rest—suddenly didn't seem so important. They had all been so confident that nothing bad would happen. They were wrong. "I didn't mean for all of this to happen," Chess said, his voice cracking.

"Well, it did," Carter replied flatly. "And now you have to face the consequences. You're going to learn what it means to take responsibility for your actions. Your grandfather built that shop so it has meaning to both your mother and your grandmother."

The thought of rebuilding the store, of seeing his grandmother and knowing he had destroyed something she cared about, made his stomach twist with guilt.

The rest of the ride home was quiet, the tension still thick between them. Chess stared out the window, watching the familiar landscape pass by, feeling more lost than ever. He wished his father wouldn't be so strict.

He'd talk to his friends and see if their parents were so harsh.

CHAPTER 20

Christina stood at the window, her smile growing as the hire car pulled up outside the house. This summer was already starting to feel like a gift, with all her children finally coming together under one roof. It had been too long since she'd had Grace here, and the sense of fulfilment that washed over her was overwhelming. The twins burst through the front door, racing down the path with their usual boundless energy.

"Grace! Grace!" they called in unison, practically bouncing with excitement.

Christina watched as Grace stepped out of the car, her eldest daughter's face lighting up as the twins collided with her in their enthusiasm. She couldn't help but chuckle at their exuberance as they immediately grabbed Grace's bags, chattering non-stop about everything she'd missed.

"You have to see the new lamb," Olivia, the more talkative of the twins, exclaimed.

"It's the cutest thing ever," Anna added.

Everything felt right in that moment—simple, harmonious, perfect. But in the back of her mind, Christina couldn't help but think about Matthew. She'd asked everyone not to mention him just yet, hoping to avoid any unnecessary tension on Grace's first day home. She wanted to give her daughter time to settle in before facing those inevitable questions.

As Grace entered the house, Christina enveloped her in a warm hug. "Welcome home, sweetheart."

"Thanks, Christina," Grace replied, her voice muffled against Christina's shoulder.

The twins, still clutching Grace's bags, bounced impatiently. "Can we show her to her room? Please?"

Christina nodded, and they immediately whisked Grace away up the stairs, their excited voices echoing through the house. Grace followed them, letting their enthusiasm carry her along despite her obvious fatigue from the journey.

In her bedroom, Grace stood quietly, watching as the twins continued their whirlwind of activity, helping her unpack. Through the window, she could see her hire car moving down the driveway, a stark reminder of the distance she'd traveled—not just physically, but emotionally—to be here with her family again.

Yet beneath the surface of this perfect homecoming, Grace felt herself tensing, waiting for the inevitable moment when someone would bring up Matthew. She found herself watching their faces as they chatted, bracing herself each time they started a new sentence. The twins had never been ones to hold back their questions, and they must be curious. But so far, they'd stuck to safer topics—her journey, their school adventures, and that new lamb they couldn't stop talking about.

"The lamb has the sweetest face," Olivia was saying as she helped fold clothes. "And when it runs—"

"It wobbles!" Anna interrupted, demonstrating with an exaggerated wiggle that made Grace laugh despite her anxiety.

"I can't wait to see it." As she methodically placed her clothes in the old oak dresser, Grace kept stealing glances at her siblings, wondering if they'd been told not to mention him. The careful way they spoke, dancing around certain topics, made her suspect Christina had probably asked them to avoid the subject altogether. She wasn't sure whether to feel relieved or more anxious about the inevitable moment when his name would finally come up.

She'd spent the entire journey rehearsing what she'd say when those questions came, but now the prepared answers felt stuck in her throat.

Finally, Christina appeared in the doorway. "Alright, you two," she said to the twins. "Give your sister some space to settle in." She shooed them out despite their protests, then sat beside Grace on the bed.

Grace's heart raced. This was it—surely now they would talk about him. But Christina surprised her by mentioning something else entirely.

"Leonie wrote to me a little while ago," Christina said carefully.

"I didn't know she wrote to you. She probably thought I'd be cross with her and that's why she didn't say anything. Before you ask, and I know you will, I'm through with Matthew. It would be best if I never saw him again. He is in the past." The words rushed out before she could second-guess them.

"I think that's a good idea. You've given things enough time."

"I've been waiting all morning for someone to ask about him," Grace confessed, twisting her fingers in her lap. "I kept thinking any minute now, someone would bring him up. I had all these answers prepared..."

"I thought you might need a little time to settle in first. The questions will come, Grace. You know how curious the twins are—they can't hold back forever."

"I know." Grace managed a small smile. "I just... I want to get it over with, you know? Like pulling off a bandage."

Christina took her hand. "Would you rather I told them it's okay to ask? Or would you prefer to wait?"

"Maybe... maybe let them ask when they're ready. At least then it'll be natural." Grace squeezed Christina's hand. "I just don't want to spend the whole summer tiptoeing around it."

"Fair enough. Though I hope you know you don't have to answer anything you don't want to."

"I know." Grace smiled more genuinely this time. "Right now, I'd rather hear about this lamb the twins keep mentioning. They've told me everything except what color it is."

Christina laughed, her eyes twinkling. "Oh, just wait until you see it. Come down when you're ready—I'm sure they're bursting to show you. I'm just so glad you're here."

"Me too." Grace turned back to her unpacking as Christina left. The anxiety about Matthew wasn't gone, but it felt more manageable now. At least she didn't have to pretend everything was fine. One hurdle was over, but now she had to see Matthew. She wouldn't be able to avoid him all summer.

CHAPTER 21

THE FOLLOWING night after the incident, Wilma cleared the dishes after supper. Iris stood, ready to help, but Wilma waved her off with a warm smile. "Go sit out on the porch where it's cooler," she said. "Not much left to do here, anyway." Iris hesitated for a moment, but Wilma insisted. "Go on now. There's not enough work for both of us."

With a small nod, Iris turned, making her way toward the porch.

Matthew had already stepped out onto the wooden porch, letting the screen door swing shut behind him. He settled into one of the creaky wooden chairs, stretching his legs out in front of him. The air outside was cool, a welcome change from the warmth of the kitchen.

Iris sat in the chair next to him. The quiet settled around them, broken only by the chirping of crickets and the soft rustling of leaves in the wind.

"How are you doing, Iris?"

"I love it here, but I miss my cat. At home, he'd always come sit on my lap after supper."

Matthew glanced over. "Why don't you bring him here?"

"Grandma doesn't like pets." Iris sighed, picking at a loose thread on her sleeve. "And even if she did, Mom wouldn't let me. She thinks it'll cause too much trouble."

"You know, Wilma loved Red—her old dog. I think she'd love to have a pet around again."

"Yeah, I remember Red." Iris smiled at the memory. "He was such a good dog." The conversation lapsed into silence again. Iris found her thoughts drifting back, when she had broken down. The embarrassment of losing control like that still stung. "I'm sorry about the other day," she said quietly. "About crying, I mean. I didn't mean to make things awkward."

Matthew shook his head. "Don't worry about it, Iris. Everyone needs a friend sometimes."

"Yeah, I guess they do." She looked out at the darkening yard. "I thought it'd be quiet here, but thanks to my brother hanging around it hasn't been quiet at all."

"Chess does have a way of keeping things interesting," Matthew agreed.

Iris found herself relaxing, the tension from earlier slowly easing from her shoulders.

"You've been through a lot with all that Chess did," Matthew said eventually. "But you're handling it well."

The words caught her by surprise. "Thanks," she said quietly, grateful for the growing darkness that hid the flush in her cheeks.

They sat in silence until the sound of Wilma moving around inside the house faded away. The night air had grown even cooler, and Iris found herself grateful for the simple comfort of friendship, for having someone who understood without needing every thought explained.

In the distance, an owl called, its voice carrying across the quiet orchard. Tomorrow would bring its own challenges, but for now, this moment of peace was enjoyable.

∼

IRIS WAS JOLTED awake by a loud noise early in the morning. Rubbing her eyes, she followed Grandma to the front door, where they both stared in surprise as a tow truck was pulling away with Carter's car hooked behind it. A feeling of guilt gnawed at her as she turned to Grandma.

"I'm really sorry about Chess… crashing into the building," Iris said softly, glancing at the half-destroyed structure on the property.

"It was an accident, dear. Your father said he'd arrange for it to be repaired, so it'll be all right."

Iris nodded, though inside, she hoped her father would ensure Chess didn't get off too easily. He deserved some kind of punishment. Her father would see to that. And if he didn't, Mom surely would.

Trying to shift her thoughts, she glanced at Grandma. "Shall we take food over to Ada again today?"

Wilma smiled thoughtfully. "Yes, we'll do that. Until her granddaughter comes. Adaline should be staying with her soon and she'll be there for the summer."

Iris raised an eyebrow. "Oh, you didn't tell me that."

Wilma chuckled. "It's no wonder I forgot to mention it with everything going on."

"That's true."

A few minutes later, they were packing up food and preparing for the short trip. As they climbed into the buggy, Iris felt a sense of calm wash over her. There was something about Grandma's presence that eased the chaos her brother had left behind.

When they arrived at Ada's house, Iris was surprised to see Adaline already there, stepping outside with a bright smile.

CHAPTER 22

"I'VE MISSED you both so much," Adaline called, hurrying down the path to meet Wilma and Iris.

"We've missed you too," Wilma replied as she got out of the buggy.

After Iris got down and exchanged greetings with Adaline, the three women started toward the house.

Before Iris or Wilma could even take a step inside, Adaline's gaze shifted downward. "Oh! Please, take off your shoes. I just mopped, and I don't want anyone to track dirt in."

Iris and Wilma slipped off their shoes, each placing them carefully next to the door. Adaline straightened the shoes and then picked up a dustpan and brush, ready to catch any stray dust that might escape their efforts.

As they walked into the house, Adaline's eyes followed their movements, tracking the floor as if she could spot even invisible grime.

Once inside, Iris noticed an array of neatly stacked luggage against the wall, every piece perfectly aligned. It looked like Adaline was preparing to move in.

Adaline placed the dust pan down and then practically rushed ahead of them, fussing with the pillows on the couch. "Here, sit down," she said.

Ada was sitting on the couch, grinning at them. "Isn't she wonderful? She's only been here for two hours and she's done so much already."

"Oh yes. What I've seen so far is truly impressive," Wilma said with a smile.

When everyone was seated, Adaline said, "I've decided I'll be staying for the summer, helping Grandma with a few things around here. There's just so much to do, you know? I've already made a list of activities to keep myself busy—between the garden, the house, and a few community events—oh, and I'm going to organize Grandma's food store and utility room." Her voice bubbled over with excitement as she prattled on.

Iris glanced toward Adaline's luggage again, wondering how someone could be so prepared and organized, while her own life felt like a whirlwind of chaos.

"Now, enough about me," Adaline said as she stood up and flitted around the room like a whirlwind, adjusting the curtains so the folds were even. "What have you both been up to?"

"Well, there's been a bit of a... situation."

Adaline perked up, pausing her fussing for just a moment. She rushed back to the couch and sat next to her grandmother. "A situation? I can't wait to hear about it."

Wilma launched into the story about Chess and his accident. As she spoke, Adaline resumed her ritualistic tidying—her hands smoothing over the freshly plumped pillows again, this time focusing on making sure they were exactly symmetrical on the couch.

"Chess," Adaline repeated, shaking her head in disapproval. "I'm sure you'll straighten him out, Wilma. Someone has to. I remember last time I was here for the harvest at your apple orchard and he was hiding behind a tree throwing apples at people."

Iris's head lowered as she recalled that embarrassing day.

Wilma gave a small chuckle. "No one was harmed." Before Wilma could say anything else, Adaline turned her focus to Iris.

"And you, Iris? How have things been between you and your brother?" Adaline asked.

Iris sighed, folding her hands in her lap. "It's always something with Chess. One reason I came here was to get a break from him, but no matter where I go, I can't escape his messes."

"Well, you know sometimes you just have to let people make their own mistakes. You can't spend your whole life cleaning up after someone else. Look at me. I learned that the hard way with one of my brothers who sounds just like Chess. Now, I just focus on keeping things in order around me. It's a lot more peaceful that way."

"I wish it were that easy," Iris muttered, glancing toward the window as if searching for a way to avoid the conversation.

"Iris, dear," Ada said softly, "you can't carry the weight of everyone else's problems—"

"She's right," Adaline interrupted her grandmother. "I mean, look at this place." She gestured grandly at the spotless room. "You have to control what you can, and let the rest go. If you have order around you, then peoples' unordered lives don't bother you so much."

Iris loved the way Adaline made everything sound so easy. Her life always seemed perfectly in order, like the pristine room they sat in. Iris, on the other hand, felt like she was always trying to catch up, like her brother's chaos was a constant, messy whirlwind around her.

"Let's not talk about Chess anymore. I can see it's making you uncomfortable, Iris," Ada said.

Iris nodded and smiled at Ada. "It is a little."

Ada suggested, "Why don't you and Adaline go for a walk? It's such a nice day and young people shouldn't be in a dark house all the day long. Off you go."

Adaline and Iris exchanged a smile and then Iris walked over to the door and slipped on her shoes and the two of them started down the path between the house and the nearby fields.

CHAPTER 23

"So, what are they cooking up in there?" Iris asked. "I think they were trying to get rid of us."

Adaline let out a small laugh, raising an eyebrow. "Oh, you won't believe it. Ada told me all about it."

"What? Tell me."

Adaline glanced around as if checking for eavesdroppers, then leaned in, lowering her voice dramatically. "They're going to try to match Grace with someone. You know, to make Matthew jealous. That way, he'll propose, and we'll finally have a wedding."

Iris stopped in her tracks, her mouth falling open. The warm breeze rustled through the nearby cornfield, but she barely noticed it. "You're kidding! And did you tell them not to do that?"

"Oh, I tried." Adaline kicked at a small stone on the path. "But once Ada makes up her mind, there's no changing it. You know how she gets."

"But..." Iris struggled to find the right words, her mind racing with all the ways this could go wrong. "What if Matthew actually gets fooled into marrying her?"

Adaline shrugged, seemingly unconcerned as she continued walking. "Don't worry. They're not telling the man or Grace, so no one will know what's really going on. It's all just to push Matthew along."

"But that's... that's just wrong!" Iris hurried to keep up with Adaline. "They can't play with people's lives like that!"

"Relax, it's just a little nudge. Matthew's dragging his feet, and Grace's getting impatient. This might be good."

"It's wrong and I'm going to tell them not to do it." Iris crossed her arms, her jaw set stubbornly.

Adaline stopped walking and turned to face her. "Look, I get it. But around here, sometimes things need a little help. If no one does anything nothing will change."

Iris sighed, her frustration simmering just beneath the surface. She didn't like meddling—especially not when it involved something as serious as marriage. But Adaline didn't seem worried, and clearly, neither did Ada or Grandma. She just hoped they weren't setting everyone up for a disaster.

As they walked in silence for a few moments, Iris's thoughts wandered back to Matthew. The way he always seemed careful and thoughtful. She admired that about him, even if it drove others crazy. "He should make his own choice rather than be tricked into marrying her," she said quietly.

"Relax, Iris, things will work out if they're meant to." Adaline gave Iris a look that seemed far too relaxed for the situation. "Seriously, Iris, stop worrying. What's the worst that could happen? Nothing, right?"

Iris let out a slow breath as they continued walking, but her mind kept spinning. She had grown up around the same people, yet the thought of manipulating someone's life like that didn't sit well with her. Couldn't love just be left to run its natural course without someone poking at it from the sidelines?

They reached the edge of the field, where the corn stalks swayed gently in the breeze. Adaline studied Iris's troubled expression. "What's really bugging you? Is it just Matthew and Grace, or is something else going on?"

Iris hesitated, running her fingers along the rough edge of a corn leaf. "It's just... all this talk about getting Matthew to propose makes me think about my own life, I guess. I'm not even sure what I want. Seeing them try to control everything—it makes me feel even more lost. If I stay with mom and dad I either have to get a job or study. I don't know what I want. Everything in the community is just so simple and peaceful."

Adaline nodded thoughtfully. "I get that. But sometimes, figuring things out means watching others go through their messes too. I'm confident you'll find your way, Iris, without people meddling with you."

Iris smiled faintly, appreciating the thought. "I hope so. It's just that everything feels... uncertain."

"That's life." Adaline patted her on the back. "You just need to keep moving forward, like we are now. Take things day to day." She grinned. "I mean, I'm not getting married anytime soon and no one's meddling on my behalf. That's because I'm not wishy-washy. I know what I want and what I don't want."

Iris chuckled, some of the tension leaving her shoulders. "Yeah, I guess so."

"Let's go back." As they turned back toward Ada's house,

the conversation shifted to lighter topics—the county fair coming up, and the possibility of heavy rain and storms later in the week.

When they arrived back at the house, the sound of laughter greeted them from inside. Grandma and Ada's voices carried through the screen door, still deep in discussion. Iris glanced at Adaline. "Thanks for talking. I feel a bit better."

Adaline grinned, her hand on the door handle. "You'll see—it'll all work out. I haven't even met Grace yet. I'm looking forward to it." She pushed the door open and led the way inside, where they found Ada and Wilma sitting at the kitchen table, sharing stories and sipping tea.

"There you are, girls," Grandma said warmly. "Sit down with us."

Iris sat down opposite them, her back straight and determined. "I know what you're both planning."

The older women looked at Adaline, who raised her hands defensively. "I mentioned it. I didn't know it was a secret."

Wilma shook a finger at Iris, though her eyes were twinkling. "Not a word to Matthew or anyone else."

Iris shrugged. "I'll go along with it for you, Grandma, but I don't like it."

Ada and Wilma looked at each other and smiled, the kind of knowing smile that suggested they'd seen many young people's objections come and go over the years. They'd ignored all of them just as they were ignoring Iris now. Their expressions held that particular blend of amusement and dismissal that only seasoned matchmakers could perfect, and Iris realized with a sinking feeling that nothing she said would change their minds.

CHAPTER 24

MATTHEW STEERED the buggy along the familiar road heading to the Sunday meeting, with Wilma beside him and Iris in the backseat. As they neared the bishop's house where the Sunday meeting would be held, Wilma glanced at Matthew. "I thought I should mention, Grace will be at the meeting today."

Matthew's grip on the reins tightened for a moment. "Oh. I didn't know that," he mumbled, eyes fixed ahead. "That's going to be awkward."

Wilma's only response was a quiet nod.

They arrived at the meeting, and as expected, the men and women split up. Iris joined the young women, taking a seat near Adaline and keeping a watchful eye on Grace, who sat a few rows ahead.

Throughout the meeting, Iris couldn't help but notice Grace sneaking glances at Matthew. She seemed distracted, and it made Iris wonder why Grace acted this way if she was uninterested.

Once the meeting concluded, everyone moved outside to enjoy a meal. Iris wandered closer to where Matthew was standing, beneath the shade of an old tree, when Grace approached him hesitantly.

"Matthew," Grace said, offering a small, strained smile. "How have you been?"

He met her gaze, his expression neutral. "Fine, thank you," he replied. "And you?"

"Good," she answered, though the tone didn't quite match the word. She glanced around as though looking for a reason to linger. "I wasn't expecting to see you here today."

"It's a Sunday meeting," he replied with a touch of humor. "You could have guessed."

Grace's smile flickered, and she gave a small nod before turning away awkwardly. Matthew kept his head down until Grace was gone.

Iris stepped over, joining Matthew under the tree as she watched Grace walk off.

"Doesn't seem like she's entirely over you," Iris remarked.

Matthew sighed, shaking his head. "I'm not sure she ever really knew what she wanted."

"Well, she keeps looking your way," Iris added. "There has to be a reason for that, yeah?"

"It doesn't matter. I'm done with guessing."

"You weren't very nice. She was trying to make conversation."

Matthew's mouth turned down at the corners. "I didn't mean to be unkind. I'm just nervous. I don't know what to say to her. Do you think I should apologize?"

Iris shrugged. "I'm not sure. Maybe do it when you talk with her again. She's staying for a while apparently."

As they joined the others for lunch, Iris couldn't shake the questions swirling in her mind, wondering if perhaps this situation with Grace wasn't as Matthew said.

CHAPTER 25

Iris stiffened when she saw Chess standing at the front door early on Monday morning. His face looked a bit sheepish, but Iris didn't have any sympathy for him after everything that had happened. She was about to tell him to leave when Grandma came up beside her.

"Come on in, Chess," Wilma said, opening the door wide.

Iris reluctantly stepped back, crossing her arms as he walked inside. They led him into the kitchen, where Matthew was finishing a late breakfast.

Matthew glanced up, surprised to see Chess there. He set down his fork, his plate still half-full with eggs and toast.

Chess fidgeted, shoving his hands into his pockets. "My father is making me rebuild the shop, but what do I know about that kind of stuff? I'm just a kid. He's being unreasonable." He sat down heavily opposite Matthew.

Iris stifled a laugh. She almost felt a little satisfied seeing him squirm. It was about time he learned that actions had consequences.

Wilma sat down beside him and put her hand on his shoulder, then looked at Matthew. "Where should he start? Can you give him guidance?"

Matthew finished his mouthful, taking his time as he considered the question. "I'll do better than that. I'll get some men together to help. We'll show you what to do, and we'll all pitch in."

Chess perked up. "Really?"

"Yes, but you'll still need to do a lot of the hard work yourself," Matthew said, pushing his plate aside. "This is your responsibility, and it'll be a good opportunity for you to learn some new skills."

Chess's brow furrowed. "What kind of skills?"

"Building, and handling tools," Matthew said with a grin. He leaned forward, resting his elbows on the table. "First thing we'll need to do is clear the debris and salvage what we can. Eli Yoder is good with wood. He'll know which beams we can reuse. No sense wasting good lumber."

"That sounds like a lot of work," Chess mumbled.

"Work builds character. We'll need to check the foundation first, make sure it's still solid. Then we can start on the frame. Samuel Miller's been building longer than you've been alive and he knows every trick there is for getting the angles just right without fancy tools."

Chess shifted uncomfortably in his chair. "Okay, but it's not like I'll ever need these skills again. I'm going to be a business man like Dad." Then his eyes wandered over to the bread on the counter. "Is that fresh bread?"

A SUMMER OF DISCOVERY

"When you're a business man, you might need to know if you're getting fair bids on building projects. Or understand what your tenants need for repairs. Even a businessman needs to understand good craftsmanship," Matthew said.

"Maybe." Chess didn't seem interested. Not one bit.

Matthew took a sip of his coffee. "Besides, working alongside the men, you'll learn more than just building. You'll learn about community, about helping others and accepting help when you need it."

"Iris, why don't you butter Chess some of that warm bread?" Wilma suggested.

Iris's stomach twisted. The last thing she wanted to do was wait on her brother, especially after the trouble he'd caused. She hesitated, but Wilma gave her a pointed look.

With a sigh, she walked over to the counter, grabbed the loaf, and started slicing it. Her movements were stiff, and she fought the urge to glare at her brother as he sat there, looking pleased with himself. She roughly slapped some butter onto the bread, then handed it over without a word, without even a plate.

Chess thanked her and grinned as he took a big bite. "This is really good," he said, speaking with his mouth full.

Matthew raised an eyebrow at Chess's manners but continued with his plans. "I'm thinking we can start tomorrow at dawn. I'll talk to the men today. They're always willing to help with a building project. You'll need to learn about different types of wood, how to measure true and square, how to calculate what we need."

Chess frowned. "Can't we just get extra wood to be safe?"

"That's not how we do things," Matthew replied. "Our way is

to use what we need, no more, no less. Waste isn't good stewardship of what God's given us." He raised a finger at Chess. "And if you're going to be a business man you have to be careful with money."

"Oh yeah. I guess that's true."

"You'll need to be here before sunrise," Matthew added. "There's a lot of cleanup to do before we can even start calculating what's needed."

Chess nearly choked on his bread. "Before sunrise? But that's so early!"

Iris didn't bother to hide her smirk at seeing her brother squirm.

"That's when the work begins," Matthew said simply. "The sun doesn't wait for lazy hands."

Wilma patted Chess's shoulder sympathetically, but Iris could see she was trying not to smile too.

CHAPTER 26

Grace took a slow bite of her breakfast, staring out across the yard. The porch was warm with morning sunlight, but she could still feel a chill of frustration and regret deep inside. Christina sat across from her, sipping tea and glancing at Grace every now and then.

"So, did you meet anyone interesting yesterday at the meeting?" Christina asked.

Grace shook her head, forcing a neutral expression. "No, no one in particular."

Christina raised an eyebrow. "I saw you talking with Matthew for a little while. How did that go? Did he ask to see you while you're here?"

The mere mention of Matthew's name made Grace's chest tighten, and she shook her head again, more firmly this time. "No. We both know it's over. He wasn't interested in anything more than a polite chat."

Christina's brow furrowed, and she leaned back in her chair, looking thoughtful. "I know how much time you've invested in him. Ten years…" Her voice trailed off as she took a breath, clearly trying to choose her words carefully. "It's a long time to wait, hoping for something to change. But I'm glad neither of you are tempted to try again."

Grace gave a bitter laugh. "Ten years," she repeated, her voice tinged with sadness. "Ten years I'll never get back. Do you know how many children I could've had by now?" She sniffed, not wanting to cry again over Matthew. She'd done enough of that already.

"I'm so sorry, Grace," Christina said softly. "I just… I hate seeing you like this. You deserve to be happy, and I want to help you find a good husband. Someone who'll give you the life you want."

"I just don't want to waste any more time. I don't want to sit around waiting for someone to decide I'm worth their time. I want a family, a home, children running around underfoot… I've always wanted that."

Christina reached across the table, taking Grace's hand and giving it a reassuring squeeze. "We'll find someone who'll be good for you. Have you thought about taking a job while you're here? You'll meet all kinds of different people."

"Outside the community?" Grace asked.

"No, I didn't mean that, but you'd possibly talk with people who you don't speak with at the meetings."

"I don't know. Would anyone even be interested in someone like me? I'm not exactly—"

"Don't be silly," Christina interrupted. "You're kind, you're smart, and any man would be lucky to have you. We'll have to consider a few options, that's all."

A small flicker of hope sparked in Grace's chest. It was faint, but it was there. "Where would I work? What do you suggest?"

Christina's eyes brightened, and she leaned forward, as if she'd been waiting for Grace to ask that very question. "Well, I've had an idea. Why not work in Mark's saddlery store? There are so many men coming in there to get their buggy equipment and supplies. It could be an easy way to meet people. Perhaps more natural than being introduced to them and having to make up small talk."

Grace sat up straighter. "Oh, is Mark looking for someone to work there?"

"Yes. He's been interviewing people. I mean, it is mainly office work but when the store gets busy you'd need to serve customers."

"I could do it. I helped Pa with the bookwork on our farm and I enjoy doing that. But I don't want the job just because I'm family. I want to deserve it."

Christina nodded quickly. "Of course. You've got so much to offer, Grace. Don't let the past hold you back."

Grace nodded. "I won't."

"Mark asked if you might be interested. He'll be so happy. I'll tell him when he comes home."

"Thank you." For the first time in a while, Grace felt a small smile tugging at her lips. It wasn't a complete plan, but it was a step toward something.

CHAPTER 27

AT SUNRISE, Chess stood at the front of Wilma's house, his hands jammed into his pockets as Matthew and his friends assessed the damage to the building. They talked amongst themselves, pointing at the cracked walls and broken beams. Chess fidgeted, hoping he'd get along with Matthew's friends. These men were older, in their late twenties, and seemed so much more confident than his usual crowd.

Eli Yoder whistled at the damage. "Well, you sure know how to make an entrance, kid."

Samuel Miller grinned. "Reminds me of when my brother drove our dad's buggy into the creek. Though at least he had a horse to blame it on."

One of them, John Stoltzfus, turned to Chess with a laugh. "So, how did you even learn to drive at such a young age?"

Chess smirked, eager to impress them. "My father has a few cars. Whenever my mom and dad go out, I take one and drive it around the property. Been doing it for years."

The men all exchanged amused glances and chuckled. "You must be pretty fearless," John said, elbowing him good-naturedly. "Or maybe just crazy?"

Chess laughed along with them, but there was a part of him that wanted to be taken seriously. "Nah, I know what I'm doing. I've been driving since I was ten. Didn't mean to crash the car; it just kind of got away from me."

Matthew smiled, but then turned to Chess, looking more serious. "You're lucky no one got hurt."

Chess shrugged, grinning. "Yeah, I guess," he replied. He was starting to feel comfortable with these guys. They joked around and didn't treat him like he was a fool.

"So, does your dad know you've been taking the cars?" Samuel asked.

Chess smirked. "He doesn't know at all but he's got so much money, it's not like he'd even notice if one of the cars got a little dented."

The men burst out laughing. John wiped his eyes. "A little dented? Is that what we're calling this? I can only imagine what the car looks like." He gestured at the damaged building.

"Well, maybe more than a little," Chess admitted, chuckling along with them.

Matthew clapped him on the shoulder. "Well, let's put that adventurous nature to better use. We've got a lot of work ahead of us. You ready to learn some real skills?"

Chess nodded eagerly. "Yeah, I'm ready."

"Just remember, you're doing most of the heavy lifting. We'll guide you, but you're the one putting in the sweat," Matthew said.

"Deal. I'm a quick learner. I've always been good at everything I've tried. That's how I learned to drive so quick."

John laughed. "A natural talent, are you? Well then, let's see how quick you can learn to use this." He tossed Chess a crowbar, which Chess fumbled to catch.

"First job's all yours, hotshot," Eli said with a grin. "Start pulling up those broken boards. Just try not to drive this through the wall too."

"Speaking of driving through things," John called out as he hauled a beam, "remember when Samuel tried to convince us he could fit that full-sized door through Yoder's basement window?"

Samuel shot him a look. "Hey now, it would've worked if someone hadn't measured wrong."

"Oh sure, blame the measuring," Eli laughed. "Not the fact that you're too stubborn to just take the door apart like a normal person."

Chess found himself grinning as he worked alongside them.

"Watch this technique, Chess." John demonstrated with a piece of lumber, making an exaggerated show of proper lifting form. "This here's how NOT to do it."

"That's exactly how Matthew looked when he tried to move that cabinet by himself last summer," Samuel added, which set off another round of laughter.

"At least I didn't nail my sleeve to the wall like someone I know," Matthew shot back, looking pointedly at Eli.

"One time," Eli protested. "That happened one time!"

Chess wiped sweat from his forehead, surprised to find he was actually enjoying himself. These guys worked hard, but they had fun doing it. They weren't afraid to look silly or laugh at themselves, and they included him in their jokes without making him feel like an outsider.

"Here, Chess," John said, hefting another beam. "Let's see if you've got farm muscles or city muscles. This beam's not going to move itself."

"Better than the time we all tried moving that barn door and ended up stuck in the mud for an hour." Samuel chuckled.

The work was hard, but somehow the morning flew by, filled with laughter and stories. "What else can you tell me about Matthew?" Chess asked.

"You should have seen him the time he tried to fix Miller's roof," Eli called out as they worked. "Stepped right on the weak spot we'd just warned him about."

"I was distracted," Matthew defended himself, grinning.

"Yeah, distracted by Sarah Yoder walking past," John teased, making Matthew's ears turn red.

Chess laughed along with them, finding it easier to put his back into the work when surrounded by such good-natured company.

CHAPTER 28

JARED, Debbie's adult son, walked into Ada's house, his voice booming with his usual energy. "How's my favorite lady?" He stopped mid-stride, spotting Adaline on the couch. "Oh, I didn't realize you'd be here, Adaline. Sorry about that."

Ada emerged from the kitchen with a plate of cookies in her good arm, while the other was still in a sling. "Jared, it's always good to see you."

Grinning, he held up a brightly colored birdhouse. "I brought this for you, Ada. Thought it might give you something to enjoy while your arm heals."

Adaline rose from the couch, stepping closer to examine the birdhouse. Her fingers traced the painted details with quiet admiration. "It's beautiful," she said, glancing up at him. "The craftsmanship is amazing."

Ada set down the cookies and nodded proudly. "He's been making things since he was just a boy. Not sure where he gets the talent from, but it's there."

Jared's cheeks flushed under the attention. "It keeps me busy when I'm not helping around the farm."

"And your mother still sells her teas at the market, doesn't she?" Adaline asked, her gaze lingering on the birdhouse. "I remember having some when I was here the year before last."

"She does," Jared replied, his smile brightening. "I help her set up sometimes, but I mostly stick to the woodwork. I like being outside, working with my hands."

Adaline admired the birdhouse again, her eyes tracing its sharp edges and smooth finish. "So, have you always preferred making things over other kinds of work?"

"There's nothing like building something with your own hands. It's also nice knowing I've made something to help the birds."

With her good arm, Ada picked up the birdhouse carefully. "We should hang this where I can see it from my chair. Jared, maybe you could make one for Adaline's family someday."

Adaline's cheeks flushed slightly. "I don't have a place of my own," she admitted, eyes shifting back to the birdhouse. "But if I did, I'd certainly love one."

"When you do, you know where to find me. I'd be happy to make it. I'll hang this in a tree."

Taking the birdhouse, he stepped outside and walked toward a tree in the yard. Adaline followed, watching as he hooked the wooden structure to a sturdy branch so Ada could watch from the window. The breeze stirred the leaves, making the fresh paint shimmer in the sun.

"It must be rewarding, seeing people enjoy the things you make," Adaline said, adjusting the birdhouse to make it level.

"It is," Jared replied, brushing bark dust from his hands.

They lingered for a moment, the sounds of chirping birds filling the air. Jared glanced at her. "There's a craft fair coming up soon. If you'd like, I could show you around. There are all kinds of things you might like to see."

Adaline's eyes lit up. "That sounds fun. I've never been to a craft fair before."

Jared grinned. "Then I'll make sure you get the full experience. I'll let you know more when it gets closer."

As they stepped back inside, Ada's eyes followed them knowingly. "Looks like you two had a nice chat. You were out there for a long time. Adaline, we should go to the markets and you can see all of Jared's work."

Jared chuckled. "Now, Ada, you're making it sound like I'm some kind of big deal."

Adaline grinned at him. "From what I've heard, you're practically famous for those birdhouses."

Jared rubbed the back of his neck. "I wouldn't go that far."

"How long does it take you to make one of them?"

"Depends on the design," Jared said. "Simple ones can be done in a day, but some of the fancier ones take a few days while I'm waiting for paint to dry."

"You must have a lot of patience," Adaline said.

Jared chuckled. "You learn it over time. I like adding all the little details — makes each one feel special. Come see where it is, Ada."

Ada joined them at the doorway, her smile satisfied as she gazed at the birdhouse. "You've outdone yourself, Jared. The birds will be fighting over that one."

Jared grinned, hands on his hips. "Well, let's hope it gets some good use."

Adaline's gaze lingered on him. "I'd like to try making one someday."

Jared raised his eyebrows in surprise. "I could show you. It's not as hard as it looks once you get the hang of it."

"That would be nice," Adaline replied.

Ada's voice cut in, a teasing edge to it. "If you're going to teach her woodworking, Jared, you'll have to be patient. She's got a stubborn streak."

"You're one to talk, Mammi. If you ever criticize me, you're really doing it to yourself. Everyone says we're alike, so…"

Jared laughed. "I'm sure she'll catch on just fine. If you're serious, Adaline, I'll bring some supplies next time I visit. We can start with something simple."

Adaline nodded. "I'd like that."

Jared checked the position of the sun. "Well, I should probably get going. Lots to do."

Ada frowned. "Oh, you young people are always in such a hurry. Stay a while longer."

"Next time, Ada." He turned toward the road, hands in his pockets, and Adaline watched him go.

Ada glanced at Adaline, her eyes twinkling knowingly. "Looks like you might have found a new hobby, dear."

Adaline whipped her head around and fixed her grandmother with a sharp look. "I'm not interested in him."

Ada raised her eyebrows, lips pursed. "I was talking about making birdhouses."

"Oh." Adaline flushed, glancing away quickly. She shrugged, pretending not to care. "We'll see."

CHAPTER 29

ADALINE'S BUGGY pulled up just as Wilma was taking the spice cake from the oven. Through the window, she watched the girl help Ada down, careful of her broken arm.

"You're early," Wilma called as they came in. "The cake's not even cooled."

"Better early than late," Ada said, easing into her usual chair. "They'll be here soon enough."

Iris came in from the back room, wiping her hands. "Who else is coming?"

"Um, just a couple of people," Wilma said. "Iris, why don't you go see how Chess is getting on with the repairs? Take Adaline with you."

"Okay." The two young women walked out of the house, the screen door banging shut just as two buggies drew up.

Samuel climbed down first, while Daniel followed more slowly, taking time to properly tie both horses and pat his mare's neck before approaching the house.

"Wilma?" Samuel's deep voice carried through the screen door. "Got your message about needing advice on selling your late husband's woodworking tools?"

"Come in, both of you," Wilma called. "We've just made tea, and there's cake."

The men removed their hats as they entered, nodding respectfully to both women. Samuel's eyes darted to Ada's splinted arm, but he made no comment about her presence. Daniel, though, showed proper concern.

"That arm still troubling you, Ada? I've found willow bark tea helps some with the aching."

"That's thoughtful of you to mention," Ada said, sharing a quick glance with Wilma.

Samuel settled into the offered chair, helping himself to cake before it was passed. Daniel waited for everyone else to be served before taking his cup.

"It must be hard, running a farm on your own," Wilma said, watching how Samuel barely touched his tea.

"We manage," Daniel said quietly. "There's always work to be done, but if you plan well, there's time for other things too."

Ada stirred her tea thoughtfully. "Speaking of planning, Samuel, how are those new farming methods working out? The English ones you were telling everyone about at the meeting?"

Samuel straightened, warming to his favorite subject. "Wonderful results. Told Daniel he should try them, but he insists on doing things the old way."

"Not entirely true," Daniel interjected. "I'm trying that new rotation you mentioned, just on a smaller field first. Need to be sure before changing everything."

The conversation wound through crops and weather,

carpentry and craft prices. When Ada brought up modern celebrations, Samuel launched into criticism of the expense. Daniel spoke instead of the community coming together to help young couples make a start.

"And what are your thoughts on a wife working outside the home?" Ada asked carefully.

"I suppose," Daniel said slowly, "it would depend on what she wanted to do. A marriage works best when both people can use their gifts."

Samuel snorted. "Women have enough to do at home without adding more. My house will run proper and orderly, once I find the right girl to manage it."

"And how would you want it managed?" Ada pressed.

"Efficiently," Samuel declared. "Clean house, good meals. Simple enough."

"Life's rarely simple," Daniel murmured.

Samuel finally pushed back his chair. "Best be going. Those fence posts won't set themselves. Wilma, about those tools—"

"Oh, I think I'll keep them a while longer," Wilma said smoothly. "Never know when they might be useful."

Daniel rose more slowly, and Wilma didn't miss how he gathered the tea things without being asked before leaving.

They watched through the window as the men drove away, Samuel's buggy taking the lead at a smart pace while Daniel followed more sedately.

"Well?" Ada asked, once the dust had settled.

"Samuel has better prospects," Wilma said slowly, "but he never once asked how you broke your arm. Or noticed when you winced reaching for the cake. Just talked about himself, mostly."

"And Daniel?"

"Considers changes carefully. Notices when someone's in pain." Wilma's eyes met her friend's. "I think Grace could do far worse."

"My thoughts exactly," Ada agreed. "Though we'd better not say anything just yet."

"No," Wilma smiled. "Some things are better worked out carefully than said outright."

"A supper, Wilma. We need to have a supper and invite our chosen man and Grace."

"A supper here, but what excuse can we have to invite Grace alone without the whole family coming along?"

Ada thought for a moment. "We'll say it's a party for the young people. A birthday party."

"Great idea, but… no one is having a birthday."

"Ah, that's where you're wrong, Wilma. Adaline had a birthday last week. We can have a delayed birthday supper for her."

"That will work. And we're both in agreement that we choose Daniel?"

"Yes," Ada said with a nod.

CHAPTER 30

ADALINE WATCHED from her spot near the half-built shop wall as Matthew's crew hoisted another heavy beam into place. Late summer sun beat down on the worksite, making the sawdust sparkle in the air. Next to her, Iris had found a shady spot to sit, while Chess scampered between the workers, clutching a hammer.

"Chess, mind those nails," Matthew called out as the boy nearly tripped over a box. But his attention quickly returned to the men leaving the house.

Finally, he walked over to where Adaline and Iris sat. "Either of you know why Wilma and Ada wanted to talk to Daniel and Samuel?" he asked, wiping sawdust from his hands.

"I think Wilma said she needed some advice about something," Adaline answered.

Matthew's shoulders tensed. "Advice? But since Obadiah passed, she's never asked anyone but me for advice about the house or the orchard." He ran a hand through his hair, leaving it standing on end. "You don't think I'm being replaced, do you?"

"Matthew, don't be silly. The family owns the orchard, not just Wilma," Adaline said firmly.

Iris added, "You know how valuable you are at the orchard. Wilma would never replace you."

"That's just it though," he said, scuffing his boot in the dirt. "We don't need any extra workers right now. Not until harvest time, at least. And Daniel's got his own farm to manage, while Samuel..." He trailed off, staring at the house again.

Adaline shared a quick glance with Iris. They both knew the real reason for the visit, but they'd promised Wilma they wouldn't breathe a word. Especially not to Matthew.

A sharp cry split the air, making them all jump. Chess had finally done what he'd been threatening to do all afternoon—he'd hit his thumb square with the hammer.

"Chess!" Iris leaped up as her little brother's face went white with pain.

"Let me see," Matthew started, but Chess was already running toward the house.

Adaline and Iris hurried after him, catching up just as he burst through the screen door. Inside, Wilma and Ada set aside their teacups.

"What happened?" Wilma asked, already rising from her chair.

"H-hammer," Chess managed, trying to hold back tears, holding out his rapidly swelling thumb.

Wilma guided Chess to a chair while Iris fetched the first aid box and Adaline got ice wrapped in a clean dish towel. Chess watched Wilma examine his thumb with professional care.

"Does this hurt?" she asked, gently testing the joint. "Can you bend it for me?"

Chess demonstrated with a hiccup while Adaline held the ice pack steady.

"Good boy - that means it's not broken. Just a good solid whack." Wilma started wrapping the thumb with practiced efficiency. As she worked, Chess looked up at Ada, who was still seated at the table.

"Why were Daniel and Samuel here?" he asked. "Matthew is worried you're replacing him at the orchard."

Ada laughed softly, her eyes twinkling. "Oh no. Actually..." She glanced at Wilma, who nodded slightly. "We were trying to find out which one might be a good match for Grace."

Chess's eyes widened, pain momentarily forgotten. "Really?"

"Yes," Wilma said, securing the bandage. "But you mustn't tell Matthew that. He'd feel foolish for worrying, and besides, it's not proper to discuss such things openly."

"Especially not with Matthew," Ada added gently. "Since he and Grace used to court."

"I won't tell," Chess promised solemnly, studying his bandaged thumb with interest. "Can I go back to work now?"

"Of course. If you feel you can," Wilma said, patting his good hand.

They watched through the window as Chess ran back to the worksite, proudly displaying his bandaged thumb to Matthew, who immediately stopped what he was doing to examine the injury himself.

"Poor Matthew," Iris murmured, watching him fuss over Chess. "All that worrying for nothing."

"He's a good man," Ada said quietly. "Matthew and Grace

think they're not suited, but something kept bringing them back to each other."

Wilma started clearing away the tea things. "Which is exactly why we're being so careful about this. The right match brings joy to everyone. The wrong one... Well, that's why we take such care in these matters."

Through the window, they could see Matthew returning to his work, his earlier frown replaced by concentration as he measured a length of timber.

Chess had settled nearby, his hammer forgotten in favor of watching the men work with his good hand cradling his bandaged one.

CHAPTER 31

CHESS CREPT UP TO MATTHEW, glancing around to make sure no one else was within earshot. "Can I tell you something?"

Matthew looked down from the beam he was measuring. "What is it? Is your thumb bothering you?"

"No. Well, yes, but I found out why Daniel and Samuel were here." Chess shifted from foot to foot.

"Go on."

"Ada and Wilma are looking for a new man for Grace. You were dating Grace for a while, weren't you?"

Matthew rubbed his chin, understanding dawning. "So that's what they were doing."

Chess nodded eagerly. "Yeah, but they didn't want me to tell you, but I thought you should know."

"Thanks, Chess. Back to work." Matthew turned back to his measuring, mind already churning with this new information.

"Aw, do I have to? Can't I go home? It's getting hot and I'm sweating and I need to look after my thumb." Chess held up his bandaged hand plaintively.

Matthew shook his head. "Real men sweat and don't worry about getting hurt. There's a job to do so it needs to get done."

Chess's lips turned down at the corners. "Yeah, but I told you a secret, so..."

"Nice try, you still don't get out of work. We're all here because you drove into this building. Why would we keep working if you leave?"

"I'm just a kid."

"You're old enough to take your dad's car and crash it, you're old enough to fix what you've done. Now get to it."

Chess trudged off, looking dejected, while Matthew tried to focus on his work. But his mind kept returning to the morning's visitors. So they were matchmaking for Grace. Was everyone in on it?

The afternoon dragged by, each swing of his hammer accompanied by thoughts of Grace. He'd known she was likely to court again eventually. They'd ended things amicably enough, both agreeing they were better as friends. But something about everyone conspiring behind his back made his stomach churn.

After dinner that evening, Matthew caught Iris alone in the kitchen. She was washing dishes while Wilma mended clothes in the living room.

"Chess told me what was really going on this morning," he said quietly, leaning against the counter.

Iris's hands stilled in the dishwater. "He wasn't supposed to do that."

"Were you all in on it?"

"Matthew..." Iris turned to face him. "They made us agree we wouldn't say anything. It wasn't right for Chess to tell you."

"And it was right for all of you to keep me in the dark? To watch me worry while you knew exactly what was happening?"

"Would you rather we'd told you? That Grace's family is looking for a match for her? Would that have made your day better?"

Matthew ran a hand through his hair in frustration. "I don't know. Maybe. At least I wouldn't have spent hours thinking I was losing my job here. I didn't know what was going on."

"You know that would never happen," Iris said softly. "Everyone relies on you too much, especially Grandma."

"Does she? Because it seems like everyone's been keeping secrets from me lately. Even Chess knew what was really going on before I did."

Iris studied his face for a long moment. "Matthew, are you upset because they're looking for a match for Grace?"

"No," he said, and was surprised to find it was true. "If it was right between us, it would've worked out. We both knew it wasn't meant to be."

"Then why are you so bothered by all this?"

Matthew considered the question. "I guess... I thought I was part of this family. That I belonged here. Finding out everyone was in on something and deliberately keeping me out of it just made me feel like maybe I don't belong as much as I thought."

"Of course you belong here," Iris said firmly. "That's exactly why we didn't tell you. Grandma didn't want to make things awkward. You're too important to all of us for that."

"Still doesn't seem right, everyone conspiring like that."

"It's not conspiring, it's being careful with people's feelings.

Grace's and yours both." Iris turned back to the dishes. "Though I suppose now that you know, you can stop jumping every time Daniel or Samuel's name is mentioned."

"I don't jump," Matthew protested, but he found himself smiling slightly. "So, did they pass inspection?"

"That's not for me to say. Though I overheard Grandma and Ada talking. It seems one of them spent more time talking about himself than asking about the community or showing concern for others."

"Sounds like Samuel," Matthew said, reaching for a dish towel to help dry. "He always did like the sound of his own voice."

"Are we good? About me not telling you?"

Matthew nodded slowly. "We're good. Just... maybe next time something involves me, even indirectly, consider that keeping me in the dark might not be the kindest choice? I'm not upset. Just surprised. And maybe a little relieved."

"Relieved?"

"That it's not me being matched up. I've got enough going on with fixing Chess's damage and the upcoming harvest without worrying about courting."

Iris laughed. "Well, don't let Grandma hear you say that. She might decide you're next on her list."

"I'm scared," Matthew said, but he was grinning now.

CHAPTER 32

Mark finished his coffee and set the cup down carefully, glancing at Grace across the breakfast table. "If you want the job, it's yours. But you need to help with the books and be methodical."

Grace looked up from her toast, heart quickening. Any job would be welcome. Her mother had mentioned her stepfather might have work for her. "I'm methodical."

"It would be mostly paperwork," Mark continued, watching her face. "Recording inventory, keeping track of orders. Though sometimes you might need to help customers when we get busy."

"I could do the books part," Grace said quickly. "And learn about the equipment gradually."

Mark smiled, clearly pleased. "That's what I hoped you'd say. I need someone who'll keep everything organized while I do other things." He pushed back his chair. "Think about it. Let me know by—"

"Yes," Grace interrupted. "I mean, I'd like to try. If you think I could do it."

"I know you can." Mark stood, gathering his lunch pail for work. "We'll start you next week. I'm looking forward to it. Thank you, Grace."

"Thank you, Mark. I'll work really hard."

"I know it." He gave her a nod and headed out the kitchen door.

After a couple of minutes, Christina rushed in and hugged her. "I overheard. This is such a good opportunity."

"I know. Where are the girls?"

"Out with the lambs," Christina said.

"Ah, that's why it's so quiet."

"Enjoy it while you can."

Grace was still glowing from Mark's job offer when she heard the buggy pull up outside. A job at the horse supply store - real work where she could help customers and learn the business. It was the largest most respected store of it's kind in the whole county.

"That's Ada," Christina said, glancing through the window. "And Adaline with her."

Grace smoothed her apron, her mind still on the upcoming job.

Christina opened the door, welcoming their visitors into the kitchen where the smell of fresh bread still lingered.

"We can't stay long," Ada said as she settled into a chair, her broken arm cradled carefully. "But we wanted to invite Grace to Adaline's birthday supper next Saturday at Wilma's house."

Grace's heart did a small flip. Wilma's house meant Matthew would be there. Things weren't awkward between them anymore, not really, but she still felt self-conscious sometimes, wondering if others were watching them, wondering why they'd stopped courting.

"That's kind of you to think of me," Grace said carefully. "Who else will be there?"

"Oh, just young people mostly," Adaline said. "Some friends from the community. Nothing too formal."

Christina brought coffee to the table. "It's good for you to get out more, Grace. Get to know more people."

Grace wanted to protest that she'd been busy helping at home, but her mother was right. She had been turning down invitations, finding excuses to stay in. "I'd like to come. Would you like me to bring something?"

"Just yourself," Ada said warmly. "Though if you wanted to make those honey cookies of yours, I don't think anyone would object."

Adaline laughed. "I've heard about your cookies. I would love to try one."

Grace smiled, remembering how Matthew used to praise her baking. "I have some news too," Grace said, unable to keep it in any longer. "Mark offered me a job at his store this morning."

"Did he now?" Ada's eyes brightened with interest. "That's wonderful news. You'll do well there."

"It'll be good experience," Christina added. "Mark is excited to have her start there."

"When do you start?" Adaline asked.

"Next week, and I'll be helping with inventory. I'll be learning the books first, then helping customers once I know where everything is."

"The store's been doing well," Christina said proudly. "Mark's added three new suppliers this year."

They talked about the store for a while, about Mark's plans to expand the inventory, about Grace learning to order stock and manage accounts. It felt good to share her excitement, to see their genuine pleasure in her news.

When Ada and Adaline rose to leave, Grace walked them to the door. "Thank you for thinking of me for your birthday. I'll look forward to it."

After they'd gone, Christina touched Grace's arm. "It'll be fine, you know. Being in the same house with Matthew."

"I know. We're friends now and I'll have to get used to that if I'm staying here."

"You'll do fine and then the second time seeing him will be so much easier."

Grace nodded, grateful for her mother's understanding. She was looking forward to the party, she realized. And to the job. Maybe it was time to stop avoiding gatherings just because Matthew might be there. "I think I'll start those honey cookies today," she said. "They need time to mellow properly."

Christina smiled. "That's my girl. Now tell me more about what Mark said about the job. Did he mention what hours you'll be working?"

As Grace described her morning conversation with her stepfather, she felt a lightness she hadn't experienced in months. Change was coming, and not only the change of moving, it was something else. She just didn't know yet what form it would take.

CHAPTER 33

THE FOLLOWING DAY, Iris guided the fabric under the needle of her treadle sewing machine, carefully stitching the seam of a new dress she was making for one of Christina's twins. She wouldn't give it to either of the twins yet until she made the second dress. Through the floorboards, she heard the front door open and Ada's distinctive voice greeting her grandmother.

At first, she tried to focus on her sewing, but their voices drifted up clearly through the old house.

"I invited Grace just as we planned," Ada was saying. "She has no idea it'll just be us and Daniel. When Matthew sees them together..." Ada's laugh floated upward. "He won't be able to help himself. A little jealousy might be just what he needs to realize what he's losing."

Iris's foot stilled on the treadle. She couldn't listen to any more. Pushing back her chair, she hurried downstairs and into the kitchen.

"This is cruel," she burst out. "You told Grace it was a party.

She'll be expecting lots of people. She might not be ready for this kind of manipulation."

Ada looked up calmly from her seat at the table. "That's simply your opinion, dear, and I don't believe I used the word party. If all goes well, Matthew will finally be pushed to declare his love for Grace and ask her to marry him. Sometimes people need a gentle nudge."

"Gentle?" Iris stared at them. "There's nothing gentle about tricking them both."

Adaline touched her arm. "Nothing's going to stop Ada and Wilma now. It's like trying to stop a train with no brakes. The train has left the station."

"But—" Iris started to protest again.

The back door creaked open. Matthew stood in the doorway, still in his work clothes, looking from one face to another as silence swept over the room.

Matthew looked around. "What's going on?"

"You're invited to Adaline's birthday supper. Even though her birthday was last month, she didn't celebrate it," Ada said.

Iris stood there watching it all play out.

Matthew looked over at Adaline. "Do you normally celebrate every birthday?"

"No, but Mammi wanted me to have a special birthday this time, didn't you," Adaline said smiling at Ada.

"That's right. It's more of a supper—I wouldn't say it's a party." Ada looked over at Iris, and then continued, "Not a lot of people are coming."

"I don't mind staying in my room," Matthew offered.

"Nonsense, you'll do no such thing," Wilma said.

"Okay," Mathew shrugged his shoulders. He walked over

and took a glass off the shelf and helped himself to a glass of water. All the while there was an awkward silence in the room. Then he left the house.

The whole thing was disturbing for Iris. Matthew had to know that something weird was happening.

CHAPTER 34

Grace arrived at Wilma's house at the same moment Daniel Yoder was tying his horse to the hitching post. She hesitated, clutching her basket of honey cookies and the embroidered handkerchief she'd made for Adaline's birthday.

"Evening, Grace," Daniel said, tipping his hat. He held a small package wrapped in brown paper.

"Hi." Grace gave him a smile. She knew him as a member of the community, but had never really spoken to him.

They walked up to the door together, and Grace's stomach tightened when she realized how few buggies were in the yard. Before she could comment, Wilma opened the door.

"Come in, come in," Wilma said, ushering them into the kitchen where Ada, Adaline, Iris, and Matthew were already seated around the table. Wilma thanked her for the cookies and set them on the counter.

Grace looked around uncertainly. "Are we early?"

"No, right on time," Ada said. "Adaline, happy birthday!"

They all echoed the birthday wishes. Adaline's cheeks flushed as she accepted Grace's handkerchief. "Oh, you shouldn't have brought gifts. I forgot to say no gifts."

"Too late for that." Daniel presented his package—a carved wooden letter holder.

Once the gifts were opened, they sat down to supper. Grace found herself between Daniel and Matthew, acutely aware of both men.

Everyone closed their eyes for the silent prayer of thanks. When all eyes were open, Grace looked around, confused. "Is it just us?"

"Oh," Wilma said, passing the ham. "It's just us tonight. A small gathering."

Grace's hands froze in her lap. Just us? But Adaline had said... She glanced around the table, noting Iris's tight expression and Matthew's carefully blank one. "I thought..." she started, then stopped herself. What could she say? That she'd been promised a party? That she felt tricked?

The scrape of serving spoons and the soft thud of bowls being set down seemed unnaturally loud in the quiet kitchen.

Daniel reached for the potatoes at the same moment Matthew passed the bread basket to Grace. Their arms brushed, making Grace pull back slightly. She could feel the tension radiating from Matthew beside her, see how stiffly he held himself. On her other side, Daniel was being almost too polite, his "please" and "thank you" coming out formal and forced.

Wilma and Ada tried to keep conversation flowing, asking Daniel about his siblings and commenting on the weather, but their words fell into awkward silences. Iris kept shooting worried glances around the table, while Adaline seemed to have lost her earlier birthday cheer.

Grace moved food around her plate, her appetite gone, wishing she could disappear through the floor. This wasn't just a small gathering - it was a carefully arranged trap, and she was caught in the middle of it.

Daniel cleared his throat. "These potatoes are excellent, Wilma."

"Thank you, Daniel. Grace, would you like more bread?"

Grace shook her head, not trusting her voice. She could still feel Matthew's tension beside her.

The conversation stumbled along. Every time Grace looked up, she caught someone watching her—Ada's expectant gaze, Adaline's apologetic glances, Iris's worried looks.

When Daniel's arm brushed hers as he reached for the butter, she heard Matthew's fork clatter against his plate. The sound made her jump.

"Sorry," Matthew muttered, not looking at anyone.

As everyone finished the meal, Wilma looked around. "More ham, anyone?"

"No thank you," Grace said quietly. "I should probably be going soon. Christina will be expecting me."

"But we haven't had dessert or the cake yet," Ada protested.

Grace forced a smile. "I really should go. I'm not feeling that well."

"I'll walk you out," Daniel offered.

"No! I'll do that." Matthew set down his knife and fork.

Daniel put his hand on Matthew's shoulder. "I'm already on my feet. I'll do it."

Grace was relieved. "Thank you." As she stood up, she

looked around at everyone. "This was lovely. Sorry I have to leave so soon. Happy Birthday again, Adaline."

Adaline gave a nod as she arranged her knife and fork neatly on her plate. "I'm glad you could come, Grace. Thank you for the lovely gift."

Daniel and Grace walked out of the house together, the evening air cool after the warmth of the kitchen. He helped her up to her buggy, then stood by the door. "That was... interesting."

Grace gathered her reins. "I thought there would be plenty of people."

"I thought I was told it was a birthday party, which would mean a lot of people." Daniel didn't step back from the door or close it. Instead, he rested one hand on it. "You know since we've both been thoroughly ambushed this evening, we might as well make the best of it." His smile was warm and his eyes sparkled with mischief.

Grace found herself smiling back. "Is that your way of saying we should stay out here and give them something to gossip about?"

"Well, they're probably watching from the window right now," Daniel said, glancing briefly toward the house. "Might as well give them their money's worth."

His dry humor surprised a laugh out of Grace. Christina wouldn't be expecting her for a while yet, and the evening air was pleasant after the stifling atmosphere inside. She let the reins rest loose in her lap. "You seem to know them well."

"Grew up here. You learn to spot Ada and Wilma's matchmaking schemes from a mile away. Though I have to admit, they outdid themselves tonight."

"I should have known something was up when Ada mentioned a birthday supper." Grace shook her head, remembering. "Adaline doesn't seem the type to celebrate a birthday, and to hear it was her birthday last week or last month or something..."

"Yeah, it was a thin excuse to get us both here. They're crafty when they want to be. So, how long are you staying with Christina?"

"Through the summer, at least. Maybe I'll stay longer and help with the apple harvest, who knows."

"The whole summer for certain, then? That's good to hear. I was worried you might be heading home soon."

Grace felt warmth creep into her cheeks. "Oh? Why's that?"

Daniel ducked his head slightly, suddenly seeming less confident. "Well, I was hoping... that is, I'd like to take you out sometime. Properly, not as part of some elaborate setup." He gestured back toward the house with a smile. "Maybe we could go for a drive on Wednesday? Weather's supposed to be nice—less hot."

Grace's heart fluttered, but not unpleasantly. It was different from the anxious energy she'd felt with Matthew. This felt... easier. More natural. "I'd like that."

Daniel's smile widened, but then grew more serious. "I should ask, though, about you and Matthew."

Grace appreciated his directness. "You want to know if things are truly over between us?"

"Yes," Daniel said honestly. "I've noticed some tension, and the last thing I want is to step into the middle of something."

Grace shook her head firmly. "There's nothing to step into. Matthew and I tried a few times, but it wasn't right. For either

SAMANTHA PRICE

of us." She took a deep breath, surprised at how easy it was to say the words. "It's well and truly over."

"You're certain? I don't mean to press, but I don't want anyone to get upset with me," Daniel asked, his eyes searching hers.

"I'm sure," Grace said, and she was. Sitting next to Matthew at dinner had only confirmed what she'd known for months—whatever she'd felt for him had faded into something more like friendship, tinged with regret but no longer painful. "Matthew and I are too different. We probably always were, we just didn't want to admit it."

Daniel nodded, accepting her words without pushing further. "So how are you finding life here?"

"It's different. It's too quiet at home. I prefer a larger community. What kind of work do you do?"

"I'm a carpenter by trade, but I can make just about anything in my workshop."

"Where's your workshop located?"

"It's just a small place behind my parents' house. I'm working on a cradle for my sister Sarah. Her first baby's due in the fall."

"That must be exciting becoming an uncle."

"It is, though Sarah's driving us all crazy with her worrying. You'd think she was the first woman to ever have a baby. What about you? Any nieces or nephews back home?"

"Two of each," Grace said, smiling. "All under the age of five. They have so much energy. I looked after them all one time, by myself."

"How was that?"

Her lips twitched. "Let's just say it was an adventure." They both laughed, and Grace realized how natural this felt, how easy. Through the window, she caught a glimpse of movement – probably Ada or Wilma checking on them again.

Daniel noticed too and grinned. "They're probably wondering if they should serve dessert without me."

"Oh! I didn't mean to keep you from—"

"Let them wait a little longer. It's good for them to see their plans don't always work exactly as they expect."

Grace giggled, covering her mouth quickly. "That's terrible."

"Maybe. But you have to admit, it's a little funny. They probably thought they were being so subtle."

"About as subtle as a runaway horse," Grace agreed, then grew more serious. "Though I suppose sometimes their meddling isn't the worst thing."

Daniel's smile softened. "No. I totally agree, but I'm not going to let them know it just yet."

When she finally picked up her reins again, she didn't want to leave. "I should go."

"Next Wednesday, then? I'm giving myself a day off," Daniel asked, stepping back from the buggy.

"Yes. I'd like that," Grace confirmed, smiling.

She guided her horse and buggy down the drive, aware of Daniel watching until she turned onto the main road. The stars were twinkling overhead, and she found herself humming softly as she drove through the cool summer evening. Wednesday suddenly seemed very far away.

Back at the house, Ada and Wilma exchanged worried glances as they finally stepped away from the window. "This has all gone wrong," Ada whispered to Wilma.

"I know. Matthew was supposed to be jealous. Daniel and Grace weren't supposed to like each other so much."

When they saw Daniel coming back to the house, they hurried back to the kitchen to resume the meal.

"Sorry that took so long," Daniel said as he took his seat.

"That's fine," Adaline said. "And why did it take so long?"

"We just got talking." Daniel looked down at the dessert Wilma had just placed in front of him. "Thanks for this, Wilma."

"Talking about what?" Matthew asked.

"I was encouraging her to stay for the harvest."

"I hope she does," Adaline said.

When the night was over, Wilma and Ada walked Daniel to the door. He paused at the threshold and turned to face them, his expression unreadable in the lamplight. "I know what you two are up to."

Ada's shoulders tensed. "About what?"

A slight smile played at Daniel's lips. "Trying to match me with Grace." His smile faded. "Though it'll be a tough road to match her with anyone, considering what happened in Ohio. Good night, ladies."

He settled his hat on his head and stepped into the darkness, leaving the two women staring after him.

"Ohio? What's he talking about?" Wilma whispered to Ada.

"Wait!" Ada called, but Daniel was already climbing into his buggy. They watched him drive away, the sound of hooves fading into the night.

Ada turned to Wilma, her face pale. "What happened in Ohio?"

Wilma slowly closed the door, her hand trembling slightly on the latch. "I don't know. But it doesn't sound good. We need to find out."

CHAPTER 35

MATTHEW LAY in the guest room, staring at the ceiling in the darkness. The events of the evening kept replaying in his mind like a perpetual loop of misery.

Seeing Grace walk in with Daniel had felt like a physical blow. The way they'd arrived together, how they'd been seated next to each other— it was all too carefully orchestrated. And Grace... she'd looked beautiful, clutching that basket of honey cookies he knew she'd baked herself. He'd always loved her baking.

He turned onto his side, punching his pillow in frustration. What were Ada and Wilma thinking? Did they really believe forcing him to watch Grace with another man would somehow push them back together? Or were they trying to make him jealous enough to finally speak up? Either way, it had been cruel—not just to him, but to Grace as well. He'd seen her discomfort, the way she'd barely touched her food.

The sound of cabinet doors closing downstairs pulled him

from his thoughts. Matthew glanced at the small clock by his bed—just past midnight. Who would be in the kitchen at this hour? With a sigh, he swung his legs over the side of the bed and pulled on his trousers.

The wooden stairs creaked under his feet as he made his way down. A faint light spilled from the kitchen doorway, and he found Iris sitting at the table, a cup of tea steaming in front of her.

"Couldn't sleep either?" he asked softly.

Iris startled slightly, then relaxed when she saw him. "No. Tea?"

He nodded, and she rose to pour him a cup. They sat in comfortable silence for a moment, the only sound the quiet ticking of the kitchen clock and the occasional chirp of crickets outside.

"I'm sorry about tonight," Iris finally said, her voice barely above a whisper. "I tried to talk them out of it, but you know how Ada and Grandma get once they have an idea in their heads."

Matthew traced the rim of his cup with his finger. "It was very awkward. And so obvious that they were matchmaking."

"Matthew..." Iris hesitated, then seemed to make up her mind about something. "Can I be honest with you?"

He nodded, though he wasn't sure he wanted to hear what she had to say.

"You and Grace - you've been dancing around each other for months now. Years, even. Every time it seems like you might finally figure things out, something happens. One of you pulls away, or there's a misunderstanding, or..." She trailed off, shaking her head. "Maybe Ada and Wilma went about this all wrong, but they're not entirely wrong about one thing: something needs to change."

"And you think pushing Grace toward Daniel is the answer?" Matthew couldn't keep the hurt from his voice.

"No," Iris said firmly. "But maybe seeing her with someone else will help you figure out what you really want. Because Matthew, you can't keep holding onto her while also keeping her at arm's length. It's not fair to either of you."

"I'm not doing that."

"I know you say that, but I can see she still has an affect on you."

"We were together a long time that's why. I saw how long they talked by her buggy," he said quietly. "Daniel seemed... interested."

"He did. And Grace seemed interested too." She paused, studying his face. "How does that make you feel?"

"I should get back to bed," he said, avoiding her question. "Thank you for the tea. Is there anything else I should know?"

Iris took a moment to answer. "I heard Grandma and Ada talking about something happening in Ohio with Grace."

"I'm not sure that she's even been to Ohio."

"She must've been."

He froze. "What did you hear exactly?"

"Nothing specific. Just that Daniel mentioned something about it being hard to match Grace with anyone because of what happened there." She paused. "Do you know what he meant?"

Matthew's hand tightened on the doorframe. "No," he said finally. "I don't." But the mention of Ohio had sent his mind spinning in new directions. What secrets had Grace kept from him? And why did Daniel know about them when he didn't?

As he went back up to his room, Matthew felt more unsettled than ever. He looked out the window at the stars, then something caught his eye. He thought he'd seen some light coming from the end of the driveway near the shop Chess had crashed into. He opened the window and stuck his head out.

The light was gone. He put it down to his imagination and closed the window.

Now back in bed, the image of Grace and Daniel talking by the buggy, their easy laughter floating through the evening air, mingled with questions about Ohio in his mind.

Sleep, he knew, would be a long time coming.

CHAPTER 36

Chess huddled in the half-rebuilt shop, Romeo curled beside him. He'd packed carefully—food, candles, matches, cat food—everything they'd need for their new life away from his parents' harsh rules and punishments.

He'd overheard them talk about sending him to military school. It was a huge jump from being homeschooled to that kind of life. What was his mother thinking? She used to be Amish and the military was against everything she'd ever believed in. Maybe leaving the faith had changed her more than he'd realized.

He stroked Romeo's fur, trying to calm his churning thoughts. The cat purred, oblivious to the fact that Chess had run away and taken him along.

Military school? Just because he'd borrowed the car once? Okay, maybe crashed the car. But still.

The shop creaked around him in the darkness. He should

have felt scared being here alone at night, but somehow the smell of sawdust and wood made him feel safer than his own bedroom. At least here nobody was talking about sending him away. Matthew would probably find him in the morning, but for now, he just needed to think. To figure out why everything in his life seemed to be changing so fast.

The summer night was warm enough that the missing walls didn't matter. If anything, the gaps let in welcome breezes, rustling the sawdust on the floor.

"Now don't go wandering off," he told Romeo, scratching behind the cat's ears. "You have to stay here with me. You're my cat now and no one can say anything about that."

He dug through his bag and pulled out the can opener and a tin of cat food. His hands shook slightly as he worked the opener around the rim. Romeo wound between his legs, purring loudly.

"Here you go." He dumped the contents onto the floor, watching as Romeo attacked the food eagerly. At least one of them was happy.

The horse and buggies outside Grandma's house had finally gone. He lit a candle and placed it on the table. The wind blew it out. He lit it again and placed it on the floor.

His enthusiasm for his great escape dimmed as he looked around the empty shop. He hadn't thought to bring bedding—not even a pillow. The wooden floor was hard beneath him.

Then he remembered the burlap sacks he'd seen in Wilma's barn a few days ago, folded neatly on a shelf. They'd make a decent bed, or at least better than bare boards.

"Wait here," he told Romeo, who ignored him in favor of cleaning his whiskers. "I'll be right back."

Chess crept out into the darkness. The moon provided enough light to find his way to the barn. Inside, he felt along the shelf until his fingers touched rough fabric. He grabbed several sacks, hugging them to his chest.

He was halfway to the shop when he saw the glow. Not moonlight—something brighter, flickering.

Fire.

The candle. All that sawdust on the floor.

Chess broke into a run, the burlap sacks forgotten as they tumbled from his arms. Sparks flew upward as he got closer, the flames growing higher with each second.

Romeo!

Through the gaps in the walls, he could see fire spreading across the floor, climbing up the new support beams Matthew had installed.

A dark shape streaked past him. It was Romeo, running for safety. Chess's legs shook with relief. The cat was safe.

But the fire. The fire was his fault. They'd know it was him. His parents would be so angry. Everyone would hate him. More punishments would follow, and maybe even juvie.

Panic seized him. Without conscious thought, his feet carried him away from the burning shop, away from Grandma's house, away from the consequences of what he'd done. He ran until his lungs burned, until he couldn't see the flames anymore.

Finally, he collapsed beneath a tree, gasping for breath. The night had turned cold, or maybe it was just him shaking. What had he done? First the car crash, now this. They'd never forgive him.

In the distance, he heard shouts. They must have seen the

fire by now. Would Matthew try to save the shop he'd worked so hard to rebuild? Would they look for him?

Chess drew his knees to his chest, making himself as small as possible. He should go back. He should help. He should admit what he'd done.

Instead, he stayed frozen under the tree, watching the orange glow paint the sky. Romeo was gone—somewhere. His food and supplies were gone. Everything was gone.

More voices joined the shouting. He could imagine the scene - people running with buckets, trying to save what they could. Would the fire spread to the orchard? To Grandma's house?

His eyes burned with tears. All he'd wanted was to escape, to have an adventure like in the books he read. But this wasn't an adventure. This was disaster.

A horse whinnied somewhere in the darkness, making him jump. They'd be looking for him soon.

Chess got to his feet, his legs shaky. He couldn't go home. He couldn't face Grandma or Matthew or any of them. But he couldn't stay here either.

The moon had disappeared behind clouds, leaving him in darkness. Which way should he go? He'd run blindly, not paying attention to direction. Was he even still on Grandma's property?

More shouts echoed through the night. Closer now. Or was that just his imagination?

He started walking, staying in the shadows of the trees. Each step took him further from the fire, from his family, from everything he knew. But he couldn't stop. Couldn't turn back.

Romeo would be okay - cats always landed on their feet. Someone would find him and take him in. Maybe Iris would keep him, since she'd always liked him.

Iris. Would she be disappointed in him too? Would she understand that he hadn't meant to start the fire?

His foot caught on something, sending him sprawling. He lay in the dirt, too sad to get up immediately. Everything had gone wrong. Everything.

The sound of approaching hoofbeats made him scramble to his feet. Someone was coming. They were looking for him.

Chess ran again, branches whipping at his face. He didn't know where he was going. He just knew he couldn't stay. Couldn't face what he'd done.

Behind him, the fire painted the sky orange, marking his shame for everyone to see. Ahead lay only darkness, but he ran toward it anyway, leaving behind the ruins of both his escape plan and Matthew's hard work.

At least Romeo was alright. But Chess didn't know if anything would ever be alright for him again.

Iris was getting ready for bed when an orange glow out the window caught her eye. She stuck her head out the open window and saw flames shooting up from the shop.

"Wilma!" she screamed, already racing for the stairs. "Fire! The shop's on fire!"

She burst through the front door into the cool night air, her heart pounding.

A familiar meow made her look down—Romeo was running toward her from the direction of the shop, his tail puffed up in distress. She scooped him up and hugged him to herself. There was only one way Romeo would be so far from home.

Please, she prayed, *please don't let Chess be behind this.*

Thank you for reading A Summer of Discovery.

To continue reading, the next book in the series is Book 2, A Season of Secrets.

HONEY COOKIE RECIPE

Honey Cookie Recipe

Ingredients
- 1/2 cup unsalted butter (softened)
- 1/2 cup brown sugar (packed)
- 1/2 cup honey
- 1 large egg
- 1 tsp vanilla extract
- 2 1/2 cups all-purpose flour
- 1/2 tsp baking soda

HONEY COOKIE RECIPE

- 1/2 tsp salt
- 1/2 tsp ground cinnamon (optional, but adds a warm flavor)

Instructions

1. Preheat the oven to 350°F (175°C). Line a baking sheet with parchment paper or a silicone baking mat.
2. In a large mixing bowl, cream together the butter and brown sugar until light and fluffy.
3. Add the honey, egg, and vanilla extract. Mix well until fully combined.
4. In a separate bowl, whisk together the flour, baking soda, salt, and cinnamon.
5. Gradually add the dry ingredients to the wet ingredients, mixing until a soft dough forms.
6. Scoop tablespoon-sized portions of dough and roll them into balls. Place them on the prepared baking sheet, leaving about 2 inches between each ball.
7. Flatten each ball slightly using the back of a spoon or your hand.
8. Bake for 8-10 minutes or until the cookies are golden brown around the edges. Do not overbake — they will firm up as they cool.
9. Remove from the oven and allow the cookies to cool on the baking sheet for 2-3 minutes before transferring them to a wire rack to cool completely.

Serving Suggestion

Sprinkle the cookies lightly with powdered sugar for an extra special touch. Enjoy them with a warm cup of tea, coffee, or a glass of milk.

HONEY COOKIE RECIPE

These Amish honey cookies are soft, chewy, and filled with the rich sweetness of honey.

Looking for more Amish Cookie Recipes?

Grab the Spiral Bound, Amish Bread, Cakes, and Cookies book directly from my store or on Amazon.

https://samanthapriceauthor.com/collections/amish-cookbooks

ALL SAMANTHA PRICE'S SERIES

For a downloadable/printable Reading Order of all Samantha Price's books, scan below or head to: SamanthaPriceAuthor.com

SERIES:

Amish Maids Trilogy

Amish Love Blooms

ALL SAMANTHA PRICE'S SERIES

Amish Misfits

The Amish Bonnet Sisters

Amish Women of Pleasant Valley

Ettie Smith Amish Mysteries

Amish Secret Widows' Society

Expectant Amish Widows

Seven Amish Bachelors

Amish Foster Girls

Amish Brides

Amish Romance Secrets

Amish Christmas Books

Amish Wedding Season

Shunned by the Amish

Amish Recipe Books (Non-fiction)

Amish Herbal and Natural Remedies (Non-fiction, Hardcover only)

ABOUT SAMANTHA PRICE

USA Today bestselling author Samantha Price is known for her heartwarming Amish romance and cozy mysteries. With a passion for storytelling and a deep appreciation for the simple life, Samantha creates characters and stories that captivate readers and transport them to the heart of Amish communities. When she's not writing, Samantha enjoys spending time with family, exploring nature, and baking traditional recipes.

www.SamanthaPriceAuthor.com

instagram.com/samanthapriceauthor
pinterest.com/AmishRomance
youtube.com/@samanthapriceauthor